RUBY ISLAND

ANITA RENAGHAN

*I*f Amy Reynolds knew that she would be crash landing into a deserted island later today, she would have packed more film, and probably more clothes. She looked back at the TV for a moment and scowled at the face of Sarah Robinson, the gorgeous daytime television host who had taken America by storm. She was bright, friendly, serious when necessary, and sometimes even regal, and there was no way to compete.

"Is that Sarah Robinson I hear in the background?" Nicole's voice chirped from the phone.

"No," Amy lied, and she clicked the TV off.

"Don't worry about her, Amy. You've got this."

"Nicole, we are going to do our jobs today, and that's all," Amy defended for the tenth time this morning.

"With Bill and Matt there together, it will be a bit strange for you."

Amy moaned. "I haven't dated Bill in over four years and we're just friends, and Matt is engaged to Sarah, so it won't be weird at all," Amy said, even though she knew it might be a little strange.

Amy didn't know she was in love with Matt Cole at first.

They were friendly, although they bickered and picked on each other sometimes. She would have to be dead not to notice that he was tall, dark, and handsome, but he was also arrogant. Amy didn't fathom that she'd liked him from the start until Nicole asked her why they had never dated.

She realized that she'd had a quiet crush on Matt Cole since she'd met him two years ago, a crush that brought her to the verge of being silently in love. It was the high school kind though, where she daydreamed about him but never really said anything except to her friends, which had been a big mistake.

When Matt started dating Sarah Robinson last year, Amy wouldn't allow herself to admit that she was crushed. Sarah was the boss' daughter, and the whole country was in love with her.

"Still, maybe if you flirt with Bill a little, Matt will realize he's jealous," Nicole held out.

"I'm going to be late. I've got to go."

"Okay, hon. See you soon." There was silence on the line and Amy knew her friend was considering a full court press. Amy couldn't endure anymore so she ended the call.

She placed her camera with lenses and packs of high quality film in her gig bag along with a skimpy two piece bikini that she knew she would never dare to wear. She packed it though, because last time she was on Bill Ruby's island estate, he had gotten her drunk and she had skinny dipped with him, and she didn't want to chance a repeat indiscretion.

"I'm leaving, Mabel!" she called as she skipped down the stairs into the living room.

"You're moving out?" Mabel called back. Amy let out a long sigh of exasperation.

"No, Mom!" she said, because Mabel didn't like to be addressed as 'mom'. Amy saw it as a floundering attempt to not feel like she was getting older. "I'm going out of town for work."

Mabel came around the corner dressed in a matching skirt and jacket, with a pearl necklace and earrings, a small purse hanging from her wrist. Her makeup was perfectly applied, and Amy instinctively looked for the white gloves. She might have thought her mother was going to a formal event had it not been eight o'clock in the morning. Mabel was a throwback and often liked to dress like a leading lady in a movie from 1943, and today was no different.

"Don't you want me to stay with you anymore, or am I cramping your style?"

"I love you, honey. You know that. I'm a widow and I'm supposed to need your company. As it is though, I'm your companion." Mabel sighed and fixed Amy's collar that had been twisted up by the strap of her gig bag. "If you move out, dear, you will be lonely and forced to go back out into the world and find a man."

Amy shook her head and then smiled to herself when her mom pulled a pair of white gloves out of her purse and then shoved them back in.

This had been the topic of conversation for three months, and it was starting to work. Amy was ready to move out just to get Mabel to stop nagging her. "Mabel, I'm sorry to be a bother. I tried living with a man, and it just didn't work out for me."

Amy took her windbreaker from the front closet and rolled it up, stuffing it into her bag. She had been hurt badly by her last boyfriend. They had lived together for two years, and he had moved on while they were still together. He didn't even have the guts to break up properly. Amy had found him in bed with another woman in their apartment, and she had been living with her mother ever since.

Her mom rested her hand on Amy's arm and they looked at each other. "Amy, I just want you to find your own happiness. I found it with your father, God rest his soul, and I want you to find the same thing."

"I know, Mom," Amy said gently.

"You spend all of your time with your friends who are already married, and unless they are going to set you up with one of their friends, you aren't going to meet your match sitting around here with me or hiding behind that camera of yours."

"I know, Mom," Amy said again, this time pulling her arm away. So what if she wanted to spend time with her friends? They understood her, they cared about her, and they were good people. Was she supposed to waste her time with morons who were interested in themselves, or were looking for a stay-at-home mother for their kids?

She shuddered at the thought of the bad runs of dates she'd had over the years before straightening up at the thought of the trip she was about to take. She was wearing her best khakis today with a white button down blouse, and she was comfortable.

Her phone chirped and Amy knew her ride was waiting outside. "I'm going. I'll be back tomorrow night," Amy said and she kissed the air next to her mother's cheek so as to not smear her makeup.

"Travel safe, dear," her mom said. "And call me Mabel."

Amy rolled her eyes, grabbed her bag, and left the townhouse.

AMY STEPPED into the SUV and put her gig bag next to her. "Thank you," she said, and the driver stepped on the gas. Her phone chirped again and Amy smiled. It was one of the friends that she shouldn't be wasting her time with according to Mabel. Of course, her mom didn't mean it that way. Amy couldn't believe how hurt she still was over what's his name. She slid her finger over the phone and answered the ring.

"I'm on my way to pick you up."

"Lucy, I'm already in a car on the way to the airport. I told you that you don't have to drive me."

"Please, it gives me an excuse to get out of the house. Besides,

I wanted to badger you about Matt Cole. You're going to be alone with him for the entire day. You need to make a move."

Amy huffed. How many times did she have to say it? "Lucy, he is a coworker, and he's engaged!"

"But you're going to be on the airplane with him, so you will be forced to sit together and talk. Are you nervous?" Lucy sounded way too excited.

"No. Why would I be nervous?" Amy asked, picking at her nails.

"Because he's gorgeous and you love him," Lucy badgered like a teenager.

"I'm hanging up now, Lucy. Live vicariously through someone else." Amy looked up and noticed the driver's smile in the rear view mirror.

"I know, right?" Lucy laughed. A baby cried in the background and Amy had to pull the phone away from her ear when Lucy yelled for the nanny. Amy disconnected the call.

She felt butterflies in her stomach, butterflies that weren't there before Lucy had mentioned being nervous. Amy shook her head back and forth as the car pulled up to the office. She had no reason to be nervous around a pompous man like Matt Cole. So what if he was gorgeous. There were plenty of fish in the sea, and besides, Amy had no intention of keeping her sights on an engaged fish.

"Thanks," Amy told the driver as she got out of the car.

She slammed the door and turned toward the skyscraper. The blue and white sky reflected off the windows above her, and Amy took in a deep breath as she did each time she stopped by the magazine's office. It was One World Trade Center, and Chase Row Press had moved all of their magazines here two years earlier. Amy entered the building and showed her badge to the security guard who nodded her through. She crammed onto the elevator and waited for the 73rd floor. When the doors opened, she stepped out and looked through the large glass doors in front of her. She simultaneously recognized half of the faces and none of the faces in the office. It was a magazine, and it was a revolving door for the new staff as they moved over and moved up, but the senior level positions didn't change much.

Amy moved along the open cubicles and walked back to Charley's office. He was the editor-in-chief of two magazines, and his office was the largest one. It was made of four glass walls and had a stunning look over New York City. Amy nodded at the faces she recognized and high-fived one of the staff photographers who dashed past her for the elevator. Amy had started as a staff photographer, and it was a relentless and thankless job.

"Amy Rey Rey, you'd better stop over here when you're done with Charley," Nicole called over.

"I think we covered everything on the phone," Amy shot back over the cubicles that flooded the center of the floor. Nicole winked. They had come up as photographers together from the newspaper to the magazine, and where Amy had tired of office politics and horrible assignments, Nicole had worked like a dog and had made it on staff two years earlier. Amy was a highly sought after photographer these days, and Nicole always requested her when Charley approved assignments.

Amy stopped at the desk outside Charley's office, but she could see through the wall of glass that he was alone. She would have hated an office like that because she would have felt too exposed to everyone around her. Amy preferred the cocoon-like feeling of the dark room, but Charley preferred to let all of his employees know that he was watching.

"Go ahead in," his secretary said with her lips straight across, which was her version of a smile.

Amy opened the glass door. "Anna Banana," Charley said without looking up.

"Hey Charley," Amy said as she crossed the spacious office and sat across from him. He'd been her first editor at the magazine and he'd not been friendly then, but he had taught her a lot and they had become pals over time. Amy waited patiently. She had learned to let him finish what he was reading and then he would give her his full attention for about a minute before there was the next fire to put out. His job was relentless, but he loved it.

He was dressed in a crisp blue suit and his gray hair was trimmed neatly. He was now the father figure in her life, and he'd helped her a lot after her failed engagement. Amy loved that he still called her Anna Banana, too. He'd mistaken her name and called her Anna when she'd started with the magazine, and when he'd added the Banana, she knew they were friends. Charley was always the stoic hard-headed manager, but Amy got to see a benevolent soft side few people were privy to.

Charley sighed and pushed the paper away. He stretched his neck and tilted his head down as though he was looking over a pair of bifocals, but he had never worn glasses. "Flying out?" he asked.

"Yes."

"Need cash or anything for expenses?"

"No, I'm good," Amy answered. She hadn't stopped by for anything specific because these days everything was emailed to her in advance. Her travel itinerary was already in her phone and her advance was already direct deposited in her bank account. Still, she was superstitious and she liked to touch base face to face.

"I'll get the photos to Nicole by next Wednesday," Amy said, ready for Charley's sarcasm.

"Yes, per your request, she's your editor on this one. Hell, she's your editor from here to eternity, Amy. She's the only one on staff who can still work with film. You should get a digital camera. You could email the photos by tomorrow night and be done with it."

Amy pulled her gig bag in closer and Charley chuckled. "Don't worry, I'm not going to make you go digital. You will go willingly one of these days though."

"Not likely," Amy said. She loved the look and feel of photo paper, and although digital photos were crisper and more detailed to the human eye in some way, Amy felt that her job was art. She also knew that she got hired as a photographer because of her discretion, and she kept control of her originals, only sending in the shots that she approved. Other photographers sent in the entire digital file, and the magazines didn't always print the most flattering pictures.

Amy smiled. "Call me when all of these computers go down, and I'll say 'I told you so.'"

It was Charley's turn to smile.

Amy asked, "How's Estelle these days?"

"You have the gall to ask me about my ex-wife?" Charley feigned surprise and then nodded. "She's fine. She won't marry me, but she's fine."

"So you want to get married again?" Amy asked.

"Call me old-fashioned." They were divorced for ten years and had been back together for ten more years, but they had never remarried.

Amy stood to leave. "Well, it's a miracle she married you the first time. Don't press your luck."

"You're right about that, Anna Banana." Charley pushed his chair back as though he would stand to say good-bye, but he never did. "Thanks for the Bill Ruby story, Amy. Really, I appreciate it." Amy tried not to blush. "You're my favorite boss, Charley," she said, turning to leave.

"Take good care of my future son-in-law," he called after her.

Amy inhaled quickly and tried to control the flash of heat that she felt on her neck. She pushed the large glass door open with her shoulder and waved a hand behind her, but she didn't turn back to face Charley with her parting comment. "Matt is a big boy, and I'm sure he can take care of himself."

Nicole was waving her over, but there was no need as Amy was already headed in that direction. "Ooh," Nicole said under her breath. "Talking about Matt with the big boss. You're not intimidated by his daughter?"

"No, I'm not intimidated by his daughter," Amy retorted too loudly. She sank down into the chair that was at the edge of Nicole's immense cubicle. "Thanks a lot," Amy muttered, her curly bangs bouncing across her eyes.

"Sorry," Nicole said. "It's just that this might be your last chance to, you know." Nicole didn't finish her thought.

"To what?" Amy asked but then pulled back. "Don't answer that." Amy opened the car ride app on her phone, and Nicole leaned sideways in her chair so she could see around Amy's bangs.

"Then why did you get him this job?" she asked.

"I don't know," Amy said defensively. "He's floundering, and he needs the work. He'll do a good write-up, don't worry."

"I'm not worried about that, I'm worried about you," Nicole told her.

"Well, I'm fine," Amy said.

"You're right. Who has time for him when you're going to be with sexy Bill Ruby?" Nicole whistled. "Girl, tell me you are going to take some extra time down on that island for old times' sake."

"Nicole," Amy pleaded. "That was a long time ago and we were barely a thing. We're just friends."

Nicole looked down her nose at Amy. "Do you forget that I used to moonlight on the red carpet? I remember seeing you two snuggled up together for his premieres. And you can't tell me you don't find him delicious."

Amy shook her head and sighed in exasperation. "Matt or Bill? You just can't make up your mind."

"You make up your mind, girl."

"Really? I already have, and it's neither." Amy stood and tried to play it cool, but she was blushing. "Proofs in a week?" They snapped their fingers and pointed at each other.

"Proofs in a week," Nicole repeated. "Be good, baby girl, or you're going to sink fast."

"When are you going to get an office?" Amy teased.

"You know I like it out here among my people."

Amy smiled and moved to the lobby, pressing the button for the elevator. When she thought she couldn't feel any more confused about life, the door opened and Sarah Robinson stepped off the elevator. She often visited her father, Charley. Sarah was perfectly coiffed in a tight one-piece dress with a slim belt, her long, brown hair perfectly in place. She was a news anchor turned daytime host and was moving up the national network ladder very quickly. Amy wondered if Sarah had the network hair and makeup staff on call to get her ready each day whether or not she was on air.

Amy was ready to say hello since she had met Sarah on many occasions over the years, but Sarah clicked past her without notice, leaving Amy at the elevator with her mouth hanging open.

CHAPTER 2

Her ride was waiting around the corner and the trip to LaGuardia Airport was quick. Amy was distracted in the security line because she used film and she wanted to make sure it wasn't ruined in the x-ray machine. When the man behind her slammed his shoe bin into hers, she wheeled around to snap at him and was frozen in place with her mouth hanging open, staring up into Matt Cole's wonderfully deep brown eyes.

"Hello, Reynolds," he said with his trademark lips-parted smile.

Amy stuttered a greeting and leaned down to remove her shoes. "Matt," she said, trying not to look back at him. The TSA agent waved her forward and Amy almost forgot to hand over her film before it was sent through the machine. She hurriedly handed the bin over as the people in line behind Matt glared at her.

He was standing behind her all ready to go through, smiling at her and watching as Amy scurried about, and she was glad when they waved her through to the other side of security. She needed to collect herself, never mind her belongings.

Amy scrambled into her shoes and began to pack her camera with film back into her carry-ons. Matt was through security and ready to go before she was, and he waited by the benches. His cool demeanor and smile perturbed Amy sometimes, and for a moment she hated the fact that she still used film. If she went digital, she would be at the gate already.

Matt chatted the entire way to the gate. "This is a great assignment. It would be better if it wasn't such a commute."

"You don't like tropical islands?" Amy poked.

"I love the tropics, Reynolds. Do I get to see you in your bikini?"

"No!" she snapped before she realized he was joking.

"Touchy," he said. They looked at their phones and waited to board, and when first class was called, Matt stepped forward. "You aren't coming?" he asked and Amy shook her head.

"Come on, Reynolds. Use some of those travel miles to upgrade to first class."

"I'm saving them."

"For what?" he asked, but Amy stared at her phone and didn't answer. It took her a few moments to realize that Matt hadn't boarded. He was at the counter charming the gate agent into putting Amy next to him on the plane.

"She's my boss and she won't spend any of her own points to upgrade. Do you have a seat open in first class?" Amy heard him say.

Her face turned beet red and she tried to pretend she hadn't heard what he was talking about, but she couldn't help but peek up through her blonde bangs at the transaction. Matt was leaning halfway over the counter, his ear-to-ear smile charming the young attendant, and Amy felt anger rising in her stomach. Amy would never admit to herself that she was jealous.

She wondered why strangers didn't find Matt annoying, but he seemed to be in control in any room, and people silently understood that. It was part of his charisma, the thing that made him the center of the universe.

"Thank you so much," Matt crowed. "Reynolds," he called to her. "Come over and show Leticia here your boarding pass. I think they put you in the wrong seat." She was looking at Matt as he winked in Leticia's direction, and the girl practically trembled under the weight of his charm.

"Here you go," Amy managed as she showed Leticia her phone.

"And your I.D. please," Leticia said. Amy pulled her wallet from the side pocket in her cargo pants and slid her license across the counter.

Leticia slid the new boarding pass back with Amy's license. "Here you are."

"Thank you," Amy said with a shy smile. She could feel her shoulders rise as she tried to tuck her head in the sand. She looked up at Matt who showed her a satisfied smile. Amy felt every wish she had in the world that included Matt Cole rise up into her throat. She gulped and turned to the boarding line, but Matt stayed at the counter for another moment to finish flirting with the attendant.

"Thank you so much. I owe you one."

"No problem. I hope you've spent your points wisely and she's not so hard on you at work anymore," Leticia said, and they exchanged a giggle. Amy turned to the door without waiting for Matt, but he caught up to her on the Jetway. He boarded in front of Amy and stowed his bag in first class, moving to his window seat.

"Sit your butt down, Reynolds." He patted the seat beside his own and smiled at her. His full lips and perfect teeth made her heart skip a beat, but she only half-smiled back. She pulled her oversized, leather camera bag up in front of her and he took it easily and tucked it under the seat. "Still shooting with film,

Reynolds? We talked about this. Digital is faster, easier, and cheaper. It's probably also better for the environment." He stretched this last word out so she would know that he was mocking society's frenzy with saving the globe.

Working alongside Matt Cole for two years had taken much restraint. Amy felt contempt when he patronized her, anger when he was chivalrous, but weakness when she looked at him, and she always tried to avoid eye contact when he was looking directly at her. Amy Reynolds was petrified that Matt Cole could read her thoughts.

She knew he needed the work, and she had told herself all week that she had gotten him assigned to help him out, but Amy was finally realizing that her crush was never going to fade on its own. He was engaged now, and after this trip, she would have to keep her distance.

"I have used film in my work for the past fifteen years, Matt, and I don't intend to change now. As long as they sell it, I'll buy it. Besides," she flashed her own smile, "I would miss the dark room experience."

"Ooh, sounds kinky."

"And I still get work," she cut him off. "So, if it ain't broke, don't fix it." She was direct with him because around Matt she felt like she had to push out with her elbows just to make sure she had enough space to breathe. In turn, Matt played with her every chance he got.

MATT FLASHED his white teeth at her while he leaned over and pretended to stuff her camera bag further under the seat. He noticed her tight blonde curls and slender, faded khakis. They were headed to the tropics, and he could imagine sharing a pina colada with her and seeing where that could lead. But Reynolds was not to be toyed with. *She's too...genuine,* he thought.

Still, where Sarah was a classic beauty, Reynolds' no-nonsense demeanor and simple beauty was attractive, too. It said 'I dare you' in a way that made Matt wonder sometimes.

~

"WHAT DO you think of first class, Reynolds?" he asked her as though he owned the airplane.

"Very nice digs, Matt. I hope it wasn't too much trouble." She had decided to be gracious.

"You really should spend some of your airline points on upgrades. Are you trying to save up a million?" he asked as he pulled the window shade up.

"Something like that." Actually, Amy donated her miles to a children's charity that took kids with cancer on adventures, but she didn't want to tell Matt. She had heard enough from her mother on the subject that she should use her points for a vacation of her own. "I like to use my miles for vacation," Amy said.

He nodded his head slowly. "Good plan. Maybe I should have saved mine for the honeymoon."

"Yep, maybe," Amy replied, but she didn't want to talk about his honeymoon, so she clammed up.

"Do you want the window?" Matt asked when he noticed that she was looking over him and out the window.

"No thanks," she said as she clicked her seatbelt.

Matt plugged his earbuds into the seat jack to listen to the pilots chatter with the tower for a while, and they sat in silence during the rest of boarding, taxiing and takeoff.

"I guess I'm a geek when it comes to airplanes," Matt confessed as he removed his earbuds. "So, Ruby Island," he said. Amy could guess what was to follow. "Don't you think that it's a little pretentious?" Matt asked.

"Not for an international celebrity," Amy retorted. She looked over at Matt and said, "Marlon Brando."

"Sure," Matt chuckled. The stewardess stopped at their row and offered champagne. "Admit it. Aren't you glad you're up here in first class?"

Amy nodded.

"We can get to know each other a little better."

Amy was not immune to his charms and she smiled, but she didn't need to get to know him any better. She would be forced to take a smaller airplane out of Miami and then a thirty-minute boat ride with him as it was.

"Like we didn't learn everything we needed to know already in the frozen tundra of Northern Alaska."

"The good old days," Matt said with a smile. Then he took a long look at Amy. "Are you wearing lipstick?" he asked incredulously as he leaned forward to get a better look before she could turn fully away. He waited a beat for her to get defensive and then cut her retort off. "You don't need it, Reynolds. Really, why start now? Unless..."

"Oh stop," she told him.

"Are you dressing it up for Bill Ruby?"

She didn't justify his remark with a response. She had put lip gloss on this morning for some odd reason, but it wasn't for international movie star Bill Ruby.

"Did you pack your bathing suit, Reynolds? We're shooting on a tropical island, and I bet that the sand on that beach is so soft and warm..."

"No." She rolled her eyes in his face but turned her head toward the aisle to hide her blush, pulling the airline magazine out of the seat-back-pocket. She pretended to be interested in an article to let the heat on her face subside.

Matt was newly engaged, although she'd heard that he still lived alone. Still, she shouldn't be putting lip gloss on for him, and she felt a little ashamed when she realized that is what she had done.

"What'ya reading?" His arm was on her armrest as he tried to see the magazine. She didn't answer so he leaned in closer.

"Did you not hear me?" he asked. She tucked her hair behind her ear and gave him a look. "Because I thought you might not have heard me since you have no earlobes." He smiled wide again knowing that this would get her going.

"I have earlobes!"

"No you don't. See, your ear comes around and just goes straight into your head with no dangling lobe."

Amy self-consciously tugged on the small hoop earrings in her ear. "I have ear lobes!" she protested.

"No. I have earlobes," he flicked at his lobe. "And he has lobes." Amy had a vision of Matt grabbing a passenger's ear, but he didn't. He merely pointed at the earlobe between the seats. Amy touched hers again.

"Maybe you are both men and your heads are bigger, so your ears are bigger, and it's really an illusion." Amy closed her magazine now, satisfied with her explanation but knowing Matt would not leave the conversation alone.

"Maybe we are both men?"

They continued like this for the better part of an hour: Amy with nowhere to run, and Matt enjoying his prey.

When there were no points left to make on Amy's earlobes nor Matt's manhood, he asked the stewardess for a refill which he promptly spilled on the side of Amy's seat. She was fully annoyed.

"Jeeze!" She licked her wet hand and wiped it on her pants. He took an old-fashioned handkerchief from his pocket and dabbed at her pants where the champagne splattered, and Amy felt her pulse rise. They had spent the better part of two years working on the same projects, but they rarely touched.

"I'm sorry," he said sincerely. Amy said nothing to let him off the hook only because she didn't know if she could talk in a normal tone until her pulse settled. Matt took this as a slight.

"Oh, I forgot, no one gets to apologize to you. You really need to get over your only child complex, Reynolds."

This caught her attention, and she looked at him, eyes wide, clearly annoyed, but glad to be past the feeling of self-conscious embarrassment. His smile loosened her up.

The elderly lady who sat across the aisle from Amy leaned over and smiled gently. "How long have you been married? Are you on your honeymoon now?"

"We aren't married," Matt laughed.

"We aren't even dating," Amy added, and then wished she hadn't.

"We're business associates," Matt explained.

"He is engaged," Amy clarified and then leaned over to the gray-haired woman, "to someone else." Why she could not just shut her mouth, she didn't know.

"Oh, well, that's a shame," the old lady added, and then turned back to her magazine.

Matt pulled out his laptop. "I started writing the piece already, and I want you to take a look at it," Matt said as he opened the file and turned the laptop toward Amy.

"You can't work on the piece until you actually do the interview, Matt."

"I can outline it on past interviews."

"You have never interviewed him before." Amy raised her eyebrows. She had actually gotten Matt this assignment, although he didn't know it. She didn't do it to spend the day with him, but to further his career. Not that he needed her help since he was engaged to the boss' daughter.

Matt had interviewed plenty of mid-level celebrities, but Bill Ruby was a worldwide movie star who had stopped giving one-on-one interviews three years earlier. Bill had agreed to this interview because he liked Amy, and she had gotten Matt assigned. She couldn't allow Matt to do some sort of back-handed interview that didn't show Bill for who he was, and there was no past interview that was worth basing the unwritten article on.

"I've read everything on him, Reynolds, and I've watched footage too."

"You're not serious, are you?" Amy was mortified that she had done the wrong thing by getting Matt the interview. Bill Ruby had stopped giving personal interviews because of the tabloids and the rumors and the speculation. He had been forced into living very privately, and he was doing Amy a favor.

"He said I had carte blanche. I can ask him whatever I want." Matt smiled and looked into her eyes. Amy blushed and moved her face closer to the computer screen.

"So what, you are going to ask him about the strippers and his ex-wife?" Amy pointed at the screen.

"Ex-wives," Matt corrected.

Amy grunted and pushed the laptop away.

"What? I'm just asking what people want to know." Matt shrugged and Amy grunted again. "You've photographed him before, right? Help me out here."

"Yes, I photographed him before," Amy said sarcastically and then paused, taking a deep breath. Matt didn't need to know that she had gotten him this interview, and he didn't need to know that she and Bill were close friends of sorts. They weren't best friends, and they didn't hang out much. Bill Ruby didn't really "hang out" per se. He might call your editor and say that he needed you to go on his private jet to Vienna for the weekend to get the proper image he was trying to convey. He might request you for a shoot one month later and then move the session from New York City to Paris at the last minute, insisting that the crew take his jet for expedience. And he might flood your office with exotic flowers no one had ever seen on the American continent before.

Bill wasn't impetuous, but if he liked a girl, he did tend to go full court press. Having more money than a mid-sized country could do that to a guy. But he was never indecent, always gentle-manly, and although Amy was somewhat insane for not being interested, he had invited her to his island several times before. Amy had loved the trips, always lying to her mother about where and with whom she was going. The island was a place that no prying eyes got into, so Amy's time there was not documented by the press like every other corner of Bill's life had been since he'd become famous.

Bill didn't take rejection well, but Amy was a behind-the-camera kind of girl. She loved to take photos, but she had no intention of being in them, and a life with Bill Ruby would be well documented for the masses. They had dated, and she had attended red carpet premieres and a couple of awards shows with Bill, but as hard as she tried, the spark just didn't stay lit for Amy.

"Matt, I have actually photographed him several times, and if you come at him from this angle, you'll get nothing from him." Amy was being sincere for both men's sakes. As she read the nonsense of Matt's first paragraph, she remembered that Matt never did research in advance so he was just messing with her again.

"So you are suggesting..." he let his words trail off so she could finish the thought, and she wanted to strangle Matt right now. She felt bad for him because he had hit the point in his career when he was too worried about what everyone else thought, and it had caused writer's block. Amy had gone through a similar period early on, but Charley had gotten her through it, and he had taught her to trust her own eye.

"Tell me that you are more than a pretty face," she said and stood to use the restroom.

"You think I have a pretty face?" he asked with his most devas-tatingly handsome smile.

"You're a writer, Matt. Interview and then write, unbiased." Amy felt herself getting irritated with him.

"I am unbiased," he called after her.

"So how's the book coming?" Amy asked over her shoulder. She knew Matt had been writing a novel for years and could never seem to finish a first draft. She also knew that when she mentioned the book, she struck a nerve, and he wouldn't ask her opinion for the rest of the flight.

CHAPTER 3

The flight aboard the small charter from Eleuthera Island to Ruby Island should have taken thirty minutes. It took Amy Reynolds and Matt Cole thirteen years. They took the hopper from Miami to North Eleuthera Airport in the Bahamas, and from there they were to take a boat to Ruby Island. It was sweltering when they landed, and Amy was ready for the boat to spray a mist of water on her to cool her down. Amy walked toward the waiting car that sat on the edge of the tarmac and looked for Matt, but he wasn't with her.

"You're joking," she called to Matt as he waved to her across the small tarmac. He was standing next to a tiny two propeller, island-hopping aircraft.

"You read your itinerary, right?" she called.

"It's just like the one in the Arctic, only with wheels," Matt yelled back.

"You call yourself a journalist?" she asked. "No one flies to Ruby Island." She turned her back and tossed her bag into the car.

Amy waited a few minutes and then got out of the air-conditioned car and walked across the sweltering cement as Matt appreciated the aged machine.

"Matt, Ruby Island is in the Bermuda Triangle, and no one flies there."

He took another look at the small aircraft. "It'll be fine, Reynolds. Do you forget that I'm a pilot?"

Amy hadn't forgotten that tidbit, but she didn't comment. She returned to the car and checked her email while Matt walked around the aircraft and then back toward the terminal.

Amy used her phone to check her hair. She was on the last leg of the trip, and she was getting a little nervous to see Bill again. She asked herself what there was to be nervous about since they had parted good friends. She had spent some time on the island, and she was comfortable there. She put her phone away and realized that it was Matt's presence making her nervous.

She watched Matt and a man wearing a greasy jumpsuit return to the small propeller airplane.

"What's the holdup?" Amy yelled out the window. "We have this car waiting."

The man turned to talk to Matt and Amy got out of the car. Amy couldn't hear what they were talking about, but the man's arms started moving fast and she could tell he was getting upset. Matt pulled his wallet from his pocket and gave the man a credit card. The man snatched it and turned to walk away, his hand waving the card back and forth in the air.

Matt had a huge smile on his face when he opened the door and stowed his bag in the back seat and then waved to Amy. She was irritated and grabbed her gig bag from the car and walked back toward Matt.

"Reynolds, you take the boat, but I don't have all day."

She threw up her arms ready to argue, but then Matt balked like a chicken and she couldn't ignore him. When they were stuck with the Inuits in Northern Alaska, they were offered whale skin to eat and Amy had tried it, but when Matt declined, Amy clucked like a chicken and the challenge was on.

"Come on, Reynolds," he said, pointing to the copilot's seat.

"What are you doing?" Amy asked incredulously.

"I'm flying us to Ruby Island."

"This isn't a video game, Matt. You can't just fly the plane. You're not playing a video game on your couch here." She pestered him even though she knew that he was a good pilot because he bragged about it. She had only flown with him at the controls once before in Alaska with the airplane's real pilot seated next to him. "And besides, no one flies to Ruby Island."

Matt started flipping switches and checking instruments. "Well, we do now."

"You can't fly us there, Matt. You might have read, if you did research, that no one flies there because it's in the Bermuda Triangle. There have been too many malfunctions in the last decade. That's why Bill bought the island. The paparazzi won't even dare try to fly over anymore."

Matt took off the headphones and turned to face Amy. He smiled, his eyebrows doing their devilish pull sideways. "Reynolds, I am a pilot. I have more hours than half the airline pilots out there. Aren't you up for a little adventure?"

"Yes, when it's adventure and not stupidity." Amy was mad now, and she crossed her arms in protest. She was not going to get killed flying to Ruby Island.

"I've rented the airplane, and I've planned a direct flight. But if you are too chicken..." He let the word hang in the air, and Amy knew that he knew he was having fun with her. "You can take the boat over." Matt turned back to the console and flipped three more switches and pushed a button, and the engine on the left wing sputtered to life.

"Matt," Amy said in warning. "Don't you have to file a flight plan or something?"

"Done," Matt called back as he pulled a map from a pouch on the console and studied it.

Everything in her screamed 'don't get on the plane', and Amy decided to listen to her inner voice and let Matt go it alone, but as she turned back toward Matt to bid goodbye, he balked like a chicken right in her face.

"B-galk! B-galk!" he crowed at her, and Amy's cheeks turned red. "Come on, Reynolds, I'm just kidding," he said when he realized that she wasn't taking this as a joke. He flipped a switch and the engine on Amy's side of the plane sputtered to life.

"I'm not a chicken," Amy called over the engine, her hair blowing around her face.

Matt's face softened into his perfect smile. "It's okay, Reynolds," he said just above the noise of the engines. "If you're afraid, take the boat. I'll meet you there."

Amy grabbed her gig bag and stuffed it on the floor of the back seat before climbing into the copilot's chair next to Matt. She pulled the seatbelt over her shoulders and clicked it tight. She didn't know what she was thinking, only that Matt had dared her, and she was taking that dare. She was glad that the loud prop noise covered her nervous exhale. This was scary and she hated it, and it was exciting and she loved it. She was confused, but that was typical around Matt Cole.

He picked up a green headset and handed it to her, and Amy put it on. "You look good up here, Reynolds. You look the part." He smiled and pointed at her sunglasses and she nodded calmly, but her smile was less convincing.

Amy watched as Matt handled the controls, pushing the throttles forward as she had seen in the movies. When they were in the Arctic, he'd sat where she was now, and the pilot had let Matt take the controls. They had bored Amy with their chatter about airplanes and hours flown, and now she wished she'd been paying attention to those details.

They rolled down the runway, and as they jumped forward and took to the sky, Amy admitted that it was exhilarating. They were over the water in no time, flying level and with no turbulence, and her nerves began to calm.

"Maybe you should have been a pilot for a living," she said.

Matt nodded in agreement. "It definitely comes easier than writing."

"That seems to have worked out for you, though."

"What, you mean because of Sarah?" he asked. She wasn't talking about his fiancé. She meant the interview he was about to do, but Amy kept quiet.

"I guess marrying the boss' daughter helps. Look who I'm going to interview right now." Amy opened her mouth to protest, but she couldn't let him know that it was her who got him the gig. "And, you know, I'm not getting any younger."

His words made Amy sit up taller in her seat. He sounded as though he was settling with Sarah Robinson. Of course that was ridiculous since she was a gorgeous successful news anchor whose star was on the rise. Amy couldn't help herself. "That sounds cynical."

Matt nodded. "Maybe it is. How old are you, Reynolds?"

"Thirty-two."

"Sometimes you just get to a point in your life when it's time to settle down. When you get to my age, you might feel the same way."

Amy slumped a bit lower in her seat. She was sad to hear his words. He was too great of a guy to settle for anything, yet he was lacking at his job, and he was engaged to someone he was settling for. Amy realized that her crush on Matt might have been causing her to misjudge him. He seemed to have it all together, but if she was reading him right, his statement was just plain sad.

"You're thirty-five, Matt. What, is your clock ticking?"

"No, my clock isn't ticking. Not in the child way anyhow. Sarah and I are both focused on our careers, and I don't even know if she wants kids."

"Do you want kids?"

"I don't know. I don't think so."

"That's a shame," Amy said, thinking that he was too gorgeous not to have children.

Matt turned to face her. "Do you want kids, Reynolds?"

"Watch the road," Amy said, pointing out the window. Matt smiled and looked back out into the blue sky.

"Maybe," Amy said noncommittally, but she knew that she did. She didn't like the conversation being about her though. "So why are you marrying Sarah if you don't love her?"

"I love her," he said, and Amy was certain he did by the tone in his voice.

"But you're not madly in love with her. Why would you want to marry someone and spend the rest of your lives together if you don't love her to the core of her being?"

"To the core of her being?" Matt asked with a guffaw, and Amy regretted pushing the conversation.

"Have you ever loved someone to the core of your being?" he asked, still chuckling.

"Once," Amy admitted.

"That's right, you were married before."

"No," she snapped back. "We didn't get married, but we lived together for a couple of years."

"So then he wasn't madly in love with you." Matt winced after the words came out of his mouth, but he didn't apologize.

"I guess not," Amy admitted sulkily. "But then, I guess it was a good thing we weren't married," she added, driving her point home. Matt adjusted the controls but didn't answer, so Amy pushed. "Okay, let me put it this way. You are married and it's five years down the road. You're in an ice cream shop, and the woman of your dreams walks in. What do you do?"

"An ice cream shop? Are we hypothetically in 1952 here?"

Amy swatted Matt's shoulder with the back of her hand but pulled back quickly, afraid she might make him crash the airplane.

"Come on, just answer the question. What do you do?"

"I jump her bones."

"Jump her bones? Are we in 1985 now?"

"You're the one who said we were in an ice cream shop. Shouldn't we be in a bar or something like that."

"You're avoiding the question."

"Okay, here's my answer. I do nothing."

"Nothing?" Amy asked. "The woman of your dreams is right in front of you, and you do nothing."

"That's right. I watch her order her ice cream and I go home to my wife."

"That's admirable," Amy said, but she couldn't leave it alone. "You're so calm about it, Matt. Doesn't that make you feel sad?"

"Lighten up, Reynolds! I'm thirty-five years old and Sarah is gorgeous, intelligent, and fun to be with. Don't feel so sorry for me."

Amy tried to smile. Maybe Matt was right about this, and she should lighten up. At least then she wouldn't be living with her mom still licking her wounds or harboring a crush on an engaged man.

"HMMM," Matt said as he tapped the altimeter. He sat back and tried to look calm at the controls, but he was worried. For the past ten seconds, three of the gauges had been bouncing back and forth. He was glad that Reynolds hadn't noticed it, but the warning that no one flies to Ruby Island passed through his head. He looked out his window at the water below and grit his teeth, and then the oddest thing happened.

The ocean of water below them was replaced by a fog that came out of nowhere. He pulled back on the yoke to try to rise above it, but the fog moved with them, like it was a hand holding up the small aircraft. Matt shook his head and looked again. They should have been flying into clouds at this altitude, not fog. Matt hoped that would be the worst of it as he flicked the altimeter again, but he lost his breath as the aircraft was struck by lightning.

Matt clenched his teeth and waited for the electric shock to zap him, but it didn't. He didn't hear the crack of thunder, and the blinding light didn't flash and then disappear. The light was on them and he could feel it getting under his skin, and Reynolds was holding her hands in front of her face screaming. Matt gripped the controls and then he too was screaming.

"MAKE IT STOP!" Amy yelled at Matt, but she knew that the bright light had nothing to do with the airplane. The light was energy and she could feel it under her skin. She felt like she was falling and wondered if it was a UFO beaming them up, but that was ridiculous because she didn't believe in aliens. She screamed again and heard more screaming in the aircraft which terrified her. She thought it sounded like kids yelling, and Amy's heart panicked at the noise. Then the light was gone and they were all still screaming for a moment before Matt sat up in his chair and checked the gauges. He looked out his window and took a deep breath. They were still flying, they were still on course, and the fog was gone and he could see the clear Caribbean water again.

"What the hell was that?" he said out loud, and then there was a bang and the aircraft shook. A buzzing alarm sounded and Matt flipped a couple of switches and pressed the flashing red button to quiet the noise, but he felt a tension in the controls.

"Matt?" Amy asked shakily. "What's going on?"

Matt looked out his window and swore under his breath. "It's nothing," he said.

A young voice called from behind them, "Dad, there's black smoke, and I think the engine is on fire!"

Amy jumped out of her seat and with her hand clasped over her mouth, she turned around to see three boys in the back seat.

Matt did a double take to the back seat. "Aaah!" he yelled when he saw the boys, and his arm hit the yoke and the aircraft started a dive to the left.

"Matt, fly the plane!" Amy yelled, and he returned his attention to the controls to level out the airplane.

"It's not on fire," Matt yelled, seeing that there was a trail of black smoke coming out of the engine. He reached up and pulled the fire extinguish handle for Engine Number One. He then looked slowly over his shoulder and blinked at the three boys seated behind him. Matt's mouth hung open and he shook his head. He blinked his eyes closed for a long moment and when he opened his eyes, the boys were still there.

"Do you see them?" Amy yelled, wondering if the white energy that had gotten under her skin was causing her to hallucinate.

"Do you see them!" she yelled again as she clasped his arm.

"I see them. Let go of me, Reynolds. I have to fly the airplane," Matt said, shaking off her grip and turning back to look at the gauges.

"You see them too," she said in relief. "Where did you come from?" she asked the boys. "Did you just call him dad?" Amy asked the oldest boy. He looked like he might be a teenager.

The boy looked quizzically at Amy. She had no idea where they had come from, but they looked familiar. Amy squeezed her eyes closed, but when she opened them, the three boys were still there. She felt as though she might be sick and then she wondered if the white light meant that she had died.

"They're not talking. Matt. I don't think they can talk."

"Of course they can. They already have."

"And you see them, too," Amy said again. She pulled her hands up to her cheeks and looked at Matt, but he was moving levers and looking out the windows all around.

Amy turned to the back seat to appraise the stowaways. They were clean but were wearing barely any clothes. They were tan and each had mid-length curly hair. Amy turned to look out her side window and she unconsciously ran her hand through her own curls. There were three boys in the small back seat of the airplane, she was certain. She just had no idea where they had come from.

She tapped Matt on the shoulder and he looked back to see the boys with a face of incredulity. She knew he could see them, but she couldn't believe they were real. They were there, out of thin air. They had been made of the white light that had come over the airplane.

"There's land," a small voice said.

She looked down at the water. "It's Ruby Island!"

Amy pointed frantically as Matt turned back to the controls and seemed to remember that he was flying a failing airplane. "See? I told you we would make it," he said as he flicked at the instrument panel again. The small craft jolted several times and Amy squealed.

"I'm scared," she heard a small voice say behind her, but she didn't turn back around. Even though Matt said that he could see the boys, Amy was sure that she had suffered some sort of trauma and that she was hallucinating.

"Well, don't fly over the runway, land on it!" Amy said as she frantically pointed out her window while the water got closer and closer.

"I wasn't lined up with the runway from the other direction, Reynolds."

Matt was annoyed. He'd missed lining up because he didn't know what the hell was going on. He was pretty sure that the crazy bright light had messed with his head because both he and Amy saw three boys in the backseat.

He focussed on the controls. He'd landed an aircraft on one

engine before in practice, but that was a craft that he had flown dozens of times, so he was nervous about this landing. He glanced sideways and saw that Reynolds eyes were so bulged that he thought she might jump out of the plane before they landed.

"Look!" Matt heard a boy's voice call behind him and he tried to ignore it. Matt was certain that there was nowhere for three boys to hide out of site in this small craft. He had glanced around the cabin when he was doing his pre-flight check, and he was positive they weren't on this airplane when he'd taken off. His eye twitched, and he tried to focus his attention on landing safely.

"It's Bill!" Reynolds called, pointing out her window. Matt took a double-take out her window and saw someone expertly weaving on a crotch rocket motorcycle along a one lane road that moved with the rolling hills. The bike was almost at the runway.

"Is that Bill Ruby racing toward us like an action hero?" he managed to say sarcastically while he was flying a plane that was trying it's hardest to crash.

"Just fly the plane!" Reynolds yelled.

"Bill Ruby, where?" one of the boys chirped from the backseat.

"Never mind," Matt said. He flew out past the end of the island and turned the airplane back on a wide arc, trying to fight the engine on the right wing that was starting to die out. "Everybody hold on," he said trying to sound confident but not feeling it.

Matt didn't know what the hell had happened. He was flying a perfectly good airplane that now felt like it was going to fall out of the sky. And who were the boys in the backseat? He banked to the right and lined up with the runway as the second engine sputtered. He put his hand on the fire extinguisher lever for that engine but didn't pull.

"MOM, should we assume the crash position now?" a small voice asked from the back seat.

Amy spun around, trying to smile to comfort the boys. They were making no sense. Why were they calling her mom? They had to be addressing her because she was the only female on the plane, but how could they be her children? She had never met them before.

"Hold on," she said as she felt the aircraft sink lower. Her eyes looked back out the window and swept the ground for the motorcycle, but she couldn't see it. Then she saw a small hanger door open and an old fire truck begin to race to the end of the runway. She was glad to see the fire truck because she didn't know how long this aircraft could keep together. The engine was no longer on fire, but Matt was usually confident and now he was sweating as he wrestled with the controls. This scared Amy.

The aircraft gained one last burst of lift when it transitioned from ocean to the ground, and Amy could see two SUV's come over the hill. She knew that would be Bill's staff following him to the runway. She was sure the staff must have been in shock because no one flew to Ruby Island.

"Mom!" two boys called out from the backseat, but Amy didn't respond. Her life was too busy flashing before her eyes.

"It's okay," Amy heard the older boy say.

They all held their breath and held on for dear life. The wheels touched down on the perfectly crafted runway, and Amy was glad that Bill Ruby kept it in pristine condition even though no one ever used it. The plane jumped back into the air for a moment and Matt corrected with the yoke and then finally touched down for good. He pressed the brakes a little too hard and with one engine pushing the aircraft, they were all jolted sideways for an instant before Matt brought the throttle back. Amy's body snapped sideways and she hit her head on the window. Stars covered her eyes for a moment and then she blacked out.

CHAPTER 4

International movie superstar Bill Ruby lifted Amy out of the plane.

"I'm fine," she muttered, half in and out of consciousness.

"Just let the doctors take a look, Amy."

Matt sat frozen, still gripping the yoke.

Once Amy was on the stretcher, Bill Ruby turned to look in the back seat. "Are you okay? Is anybody hurt?" He was yelling even though there was no engine noise, and Matt let go of the yoke and turned around slowly.

He hadn't imagined it. There were three young boys in the back seat who looked to be in shock but not injured. Matt turned slowly back to Bill Ruby. He'd been secretly excited to meet the movie star, but now he found that he was glad he hadn't told anyone about this interview yet. He hated the perfectly tanned and sculpted real life superhero already.

"They're fine," he said evenly. "We're all okay."

Bill Ruby nodded and flashed his million-dollar smile before jumping from the wing into a barrel roll and landing at Amy's side.

When Amy woke, she was being pulled from the airplane. She

coughed and tried to turn her head but there was a neck brace tightened below her chin. She slowly opened one eye, and she could see Bill Ruby and two of his staff working over her. It took her a minute to realize that they were strapping her to a stretcher.

"Amy, can you hear me?" Bill asked as he placed his hands gently on her cheeks. Amy opened both of her eyes and looked at Bill. He really was extremely attractive with his deep, brown eyes specked with yellow, and his perfect, shiny brown hair barely tousled after his motorcycle ride. Amy tried to smile but her face hurt when she moved her lips.

"Bill," she moaned. "What happened?"

Bill's eyes glimmered in the sunlight and he threw his head back and laughed. "You flew to Ruby Island! That's what happened. What would make you try such a foolish thing?"

Amy tried to smile again and then pulled her hand up to her head and moaned. There was a pounding there and she closed one eye to try to make the hurt go away. "Matt was badgering me," she moaned.

"Who's Matt?" Bill asked, and then Amy realized that they had never met. She blushed, and Bill noticed, but he didn't react. "Nobody flies to Ruby Island, Amy. That's why I bought it. You know, so we could skinny dip without any cameras lurking in the bushes."

Bill's eyebrows bounced with innuendo and although he was playing it cool, Amy saw him look toward the airplane with steely eyes. He had noticed her blush, and he was sizing up Matt.

"And what's with the kids?" Bill asked. "You really lost all judgment flying here with children, Amy. You could have at least put them on the boat." He was chastising her and she would have deserved it if she had put the kids on the airplane. But she hadn't.

"The boys?" Amy asked. So they were real. She had forgotten about them for a moment.

"They're okay. I have my team looking them over, but it seems you got it the worst. Doctor Bruce wants to see you as soon as he can, and you know how he can be when left waiting."

"We'd better get going then," she conceded, remembering Doctor Bruce sewing stitches in her knee after a small four-wheeler accident. Amy closed her eyes.

"We're going in to see the doctor right away, boys," Bill commanded as Amy's stretcher was lifted into a waiting SUV. He looked to his left and said softly, "You can ride with me."

"On your motorcycle?" a small excited voice asked.

Bill laughed. "Not this time. Let's take this car for now."

"Come on, Dad!" Amy heard as they closed the doors. She remembered that Matt was dad and she was mom before she passed out again.

MATT WAS glad that these boys were here to pepper Bill Ruby with questions. The blockbuster action star was gracious to the boys, but Matt had noticed the ice-cold stare that he had seen on movie screens aimed in his direction, and it was intimidating. It was all too much. Matt was on Billy Ruby's island in Bill Ruby's car headed to see Bill Ruby's personal doctor.

Matt closed his eyes several times and rubbed his forehead while listening to three boys and a movie star continually repeat the dangers of flying to Ruby Island. The smallest boy kept grabbing his hand, and Matt constantly brushed it away. He didn't know who these boys were, and he was starting to feel claustrophobic. He took three deep breaths. He'd landed the plane without crashing, and he hoped to God that Reynolds would be all right. If that wasn't bad enough, he felt completely insignificant when they crested a hill and he saw a large resort hotel in front of him, only to realize that this was Bill Ruby's personal residence.

They pulled up to the front and Bill hopped out before the car was stopped. Bill disappeared inside with Amy's gurney as Matt and the three boys were ushered in another door. This was the first time that Matt had taken a close look at the boys, and they were barely dressed. He realized that their tropical clothes were like tattered rags weaved together. They looked like they were straight out of a Broadway Peter Pan musical, but they had familiar faces that gnawed at the edges of his brain.

One of Bill Ruby's staff brought Matt a whiskey neat and Matt drank it in one gulp. The glass was replaced full in seconds. Matt had checked his Apple Watch four times for the date, but both his watch and his phone were dead.

He watched as staff members were taking photos of the boys, and he assumed it was for some liability in case they sued for something. The smallest boy walked over and hugged Matt three times.

"What day is it?" Matt asked three different people. They all answered correctly and this was the exact date he and Reynolds had flown from New York City to meet Bill Ruby. But these boys had literally appeared out of nowhere and they were calling him dad. They knew him, he could see it in their eyes. Matt held up his glass for another refill. He was losing his mind.

"We will have your sons cleaned up and changed into fresh clothes in no time," one of the staff told him as she brought Matt a fresh glass.

"They aren't mine," he cringed. "I don't know who they are."

She smiled courteously. "Maybe I'd better not refill your glass anymore," she said with a wink.

"They're not mine," Matt said again, this time under his breath. He went through the flight over and over in his mind, and they had appeared out of thin air. Reynolds had seen them too, and this staff and Bill Ruby could see them, so he knew they were real. He just couldn't account for their sudden existence on the airplane.

In less than ten minutes, clean outfits were brought down,

and the boys were ushered to an adjoining room to change. Actually, they would have each been escorted to their own rooms, but they insisted on staying together and the staff was forced to relent. Matt gulped his whiskey again, and the boys soon returned in their new outfits, their hair perfectly coiffed, and more photos taken.

He should never have insisted on flying to Ruby Island. He was being a stupid show-off. What would Sarah care if he were back in one day or two? She had plenty to keep her busy, and she could live on gossip about his meeting with Bill Ruby for months. He put the glass down on a side table and noticed that his hands were shaking, so he sat down and pushed them under his knees so no one else would notice.

A giant, black man with long dreadlocks stepped into the room from a large door. He looked over the kids, and squinted at Matt for a moment before turning back to hold the door open. Bill Ruby swept into the room, and Matt stood. The bodyguard took a step forward, but Ruby shook his head in a minuscule gesture that the guard caught, and he faded back to the door.

Matt watched as the staff moved about Bill Ruby like worker bees. They were doing his bidding without words. It was creepy, like the Borg in Star Trek. Matt shuddered as Bill Ruby stopped in front of him.

He was a tiny man; a full foot shorter than Matt and his frame was slight but muscular. Matt couldn't believe that this was the hero movie star of so many action blockbusters. He might have laughed out loud if he wasn't so nervous.

"So, you're Matt Cole," Bill Ruby said straight-faced. Matt stood silently until Bill thrust his hand forward, with a massive smile spreading across his face. Matt couldn't help but smile too, and he shook Bill's hand in greeting.

"Mr. Ruby, thank you so much for granting me this interview."

The little man crushed Matt's grip as the three boys came forward.

"You really are Bill Ruby?" they cawed together. The superstar laughed and turned his attention to the boys, and Matt was relieved.

"And what are your names?" Ruby asked.

"I'm Bill. My parents named me after you," the oldest one said, shrinking back in embarrassment.

"Well, that's quite an honor," Bill said, and he shook the boy's hand, and Matt noticed that they were the same height when the boy stood up straight.

"I'm Steven, and this is Benji," the middle boy said. Steven shook Bill Ruby's hand, smiling and looking up into his face like he was a god. Benji tried to hide behind Steven, but Ruby side-stepped and leaned down.

"Do you know how to shake hands like your brothers do?" he asked the frightened boy.

Matt felt the urge to pick Ruby up and fling him across the room, and dreadlocks must have read his mind because he actually took a step forward. "He's just shy," Matt said calmly, not knowing what came over him. Ruby ignored Matt.

"Here you go," the movie star said calmly. "You just put your hand out like this," the boy mimicked Ruby until their hands were together. "And you do a nice firm shake, and then that's it." The boy smiled up at Bill Ruby, and Matt's blood boiled.

The guard turned to the door and opened it, and Reynolds was escorted into the room by a doctor and a nurse. She still had the neck brace on accompanied by two small Band-Aids on her face. Bill Ruby was across the room in an instant, and he took her hands. He kissed her on both cheeks and then gave her a peck on the lips. Matt expected Reynolds to slap his face, but she didn't. She smiled at Ruby and put her hand on his cheek for a moment before noticing everyone else in the room.

"You know each other well?" Matt asked, completely

confused. The oldest boy moved to stand next to Reynolds, taking her hand and trying to pry a wedge between her and Bill Ruby. The other boys moved to Reynolds and hugged her, and she was uncomfortable as she patted their backs. Matt could see the oldest boy looking at him as though he should be stepping in, and it made him uncomfortable, so he ignored it. Still, he couldn't ignore how comfortable Reynolds was with Bill Ruby.

"She's the one that got away," Ruby said, not taking his eyes from Reynolds. "Put that in your article."

"Don't put that in your article," Reynolds called and then grabbed her neck.

"Doc?" Ruby asked.

"She'll be just fine," the doctor answered. "Give her some room, boys," he said, and the three boys melted back toward Matt. "The CAT scan showed no concussion, but she does have some whiplash, and I don't think she should travel for at least two days. The neck brace should be used for forty-eight hours, and I'd like to keep an eye on her. She's had some pain killers, and I filled a prescription for the week." Bill nodded, and Reynolds thanked them, and the doctor and nurse left the room.

Matt's mouth was hanging open, but he didn't know it. He was even more baffled by the staff on this island. It seemed that it was a small city put together for one man's use.

"How's Mabel?" Ruby asked.

"She's the same," Reynolds said.

"I bet she is," Ruby said with a laugh. "Do you want to call her and let her know you have arrived safely?"

"I'll call her later," Reynolds said. "She expects me back tomorrow."

"Well you heard the Doc, you're staying for at least two days."

"Who's Mabel?" Matt asked.

"That's Mom's mother," the oldest boy said, and all three adults in the room turned to stare at him.

"That's right!" Reynolds said in excited surprise, and the painkillers were obviously doing their job.

The guard turned to open the door again, and a black-tied butler entered the room. Matt leaned sideways and looked into the bodyguard's ear, but he didn't see a communication device. *How does he always know when someone is about to enter?* he thought. It was another creepy thing about this place.

"Lunch is served, Mr. Ruby," the butler said and stepped aside to let the guests pass.

"It's nice to see you again, Mr. Donnelly," Reynolds said as Ruby took her elbow to escort her from the room.

"Miss Reynolds," the butler said with a nod.

"Reynolds, can we talk?" Matt asked and all heads turned to look at him.

"Go ahead and eat," she said, and Donnelly escorted the three boys out, but Bill Ruby remained to Matt's annoyance.

"I want to talk about the boys," Matt said through clenched teeth and looked between Reynolds and Ruby.

"They seem to be just fine," Bill Ruby said. "Let's not worry Amy. She needs to rest and relax."

"It's okay," she said to Bill, the pleasant pain killers receding into the background of her mind as she tried to focus.

"Where did they come from?" Matt asked Reynolds.

"Do we need to talk about the birds and the bees?" Ruby quipped and then chuckled.

"I don't know, Matt. There was that crazy flash of light, and then they were there," Reynolds said.

The butler returned and cleared his throat, and Matt woke from his stupor.

"The boys aren't sure what they should eat," he told Matt.

"The boys," Amy said with a look of worry on her face. Matt tried to relax when Bill Ruby took Amy's arm and turned her toward the hall. He didn't know if it was Bill Ruby that upset him, or if it was the boys, but he wanted to scream at everyone to leave him alone with Reynolds long enough to have a conversation.

The butler extended his arm and then followed Matt down the massive hallway to a large dining room. The huge, wooden table was immaculately polished to show off the yellow tones in the light, brown wood. There was a large buffet along the back of the room with food for at least ten people on it.

The three boys were staring at the food. Reynolds was behind them, and she grabbed a plate and handed it to the oldest. "Help yourself," she said. "If you aren't sure what to eat, just try a little bit."

Bill Ruby pulled out a chair next to the head of the table. "Amy, don't exert yourself. Donnelly will take care of everyone." As soon as he'd said it, two other servants appeared and moved down the buffet line with the children. The boys asked what everything was, and they helped themselves to heaping plates filled with at least one of everything. Matt watched as Ruby made a plate for himself, choosing carefully. Then Matt gulped back his ire when he saw Bill Ruby place the plate in front of Reynolds.

"You remember," she said with a smile.

"Of course," Bill Ruby said as he sat down next to her. Donnelly swept in with a plate for Ruby and the boys got settled in around them. "Please, Matt, help yourself," Ruby said. The kids dug into their food, and Ruby laughed. "Don't mind us if we start without you."

Matt walked unsteadily to the buffet where a servant held a plate for him. He randomly pointed at the gourmet cold and cooked fish, salads, and fruit. He was stunned that they could pull all of this together so quickly, and he was only half-paying attention because he was trying to figure out where the boys had come from. Matt was worried that he might be losing his mind, and panic was pulling at the edges of his nerves.

"Sit here, Dad!" the smallest boy patted the chair next to him, and the servant moved to the table and placed his plate there, so

Matt dazedly obeyed. When he was seated, Matt pressed the tines on the fork into his leg to try to wake himself up from this dream, but it didn't work.

"So, Bill, how do you know Reynolds' mom?" Matt asked.

Bill Ruby nodded slowly and put down his fork, making sure he finished his bite of food before answering. He reached over and took Reynolds' hand before turning to Matt. "Well, Matt, when my father passed away suddenly, I was just getting to know Amy from some photo shoots we had done. It was a tough time for me, but Amy had lost her father too, and she really got me through a dark time." Bill turned to her and smiled. "We saw some of the world together for a while before Amy broke my heart."

"I didn't break your heart!" Reynolds protested. Bill smiled at her and Matt felt a growl on his lips. He didn't like Bill Ruby, and he didn't believe him either.

"She did break his heart!" The oldest boy concurred. Matt stared at him for a second wondering who he was and how he could know that.

"See?" Ruby asked conclusively.

"You dated, and Reynolds broke up with you?" Matt asked incredulously. He knew that she traveled for work but had no idea she was such a jet-setter.

Bill leaned onto his elbows and told Matt sincerely, "She was too good for me."

"MATT'S WRITING A BOOK," Amy said before she could stop herself. Mentioning Matt's book had become a self-defense mechanism to change the subject, and Amy knew it was wrong. Still, she couldn't have these men just sit here and talk about her. She needed to deflect the attention. "He's been working on it for a long time, and he won't show me any of it. I'm not sure he's even writing it at all," she said with her smile turned toward Matt. She felt brash. It was the painkillers giving her courage, and she liked it.

"What's your book about?" Ruby asked as he chewed his food.

Matt was terrified. Here was a world-wide movie star asking him about his book, and he didn't know how to answer. He had written over half the book, but he never showed anyone his progress. Matt was sure that it would be the next great work of literature, or he was pretty sure anyway. "It's literary fiction," Matt said, trying to take a bite of food. "It's hard to describe." Matt felt sheepish. This was his chance to get the attention of someone who had more contacts in the publishing business than he did, but he was embarrassed.

"Well, if there's anything I've learned about pitching a story in the movie business, it's that you need three really good sentences to get the story across or you lose them."

"Can we watch one of your movies?" the oldest boy named Bill asked.

"Sure," Ruby said with a laugh. "Which one?"

"I don't know. We've never seen any of your movies."

"What?" Ruby asked with a smile. "You've never seen any of my movies? Where have you been living, in a cave?" He was joking, but the boy didn't smile.

Benji's tiny voice answered. "We were living in a cave on the island." The three adults stopped and stared at him. Amy's heart sank. She was still in shock from the rough landing, and the pills made everything a little hazy. Still, these boys had come out of nowhere and she didn't know how to deal with them. They were calling her 'mom' and calling Matt 'dad'. It was unreal.

"Can we see a movie, Mom?" Benji asked.

"Yes, of course," Amy answered.

"Mom?" Ruby asked Amy. Then he turned his attention to Matt. "Maybe next time you will heed Amy's thoughts on the subject of how to get here. And if I would've known you were bringing your boys, I would've planned some fun things for them to do while they were here."

"My boys?" Matt asked, and Reynolds dropped her fork.

"Are you okay, Amy?" Ruby asked as he reached across and put a hand on her shoulder. She smiled and Ruby turned his attention back to Matt. "Yes, your boys. I'm surprised you would take the chance and fly them to Ruby Island."

Matt looked at the little faces, convinced he had never seen them before in his life. "Those aren't my boys," Matt said a little embarrassed.

"Dad!" the oldest yelled, and Matt shrugged.

"Donnelly, can you take the boys to the theater and ask Rebecca if she could sit with them?" Amy asked.

"Of course, Miss Reynolds," the butler answered with the nod of his head. "Come with me, young men. I know just the movie you should start with." The youngest hugged Matt and then Amy, and then the three boys left with Donnelly. Bill Ruby put his fork down and pushed his chair back from the table.

"Mom?" he asked again. "What's going on, Amy?"

"I will tell you, but you won't believe me," Amy said. Then she told Bill Ruby the whole story, starting with the fact that they were supposed to take a boat over like everyone else, about the bright flash of light when they thought they were dying, the boys appearing in the back seat, and finally ending when she saw him speeding out to the runway on a motorcycle to save them. Matt rolled his eyes at this. They didn't crash or anything crazy. No one needed saving.

And today was the day that they were supposed to arrive for the photo shoot and interview. It was the same date on the calendar as when she had packed her bag at home and had boarded her flight in New York City. They hadn't been on an island and living in a cave for years and years. They were in the airplane on their way to Ruby Island, and the boys just appeared. It was insane and Amy knew it, but it was also true.

When she was done, Bill Ruby had a good laugh at both of his guests. "Amy, you know nobody flies to the island. That's why I bought it."

"I know," Amy said defensively, "but he was badgering me." Amy's face turned pink, and Bill Ruby didn't say anything. He knew why she was blushing, but he wanted her for himself.

~

"THOSE ARE NOT OUR CHILDREN," Matt insisted.

"Of course they are," Bill Ruby cut in decisively. "Look at the oldest. He looks just like you."

Matt looked at Reynolds and she looked back at him. They both knew that Ruby was right. The resemblance was uncanny.

"What I can't figure is that they are calling you both mom and dad, and I know for a fact that Amy's not a mom, not yet anyway."

Ruby took Amy's hand and Matt could see them share a moment. This made him angry. He didn't know who these boys were or where they had come from. They had appeared after that giant flash of light and it was as though they had come from the light itself. He was getting upset, but he didn't want to show his temper. He was not their father and Reynolds was not their mother. Matt knew that for sure.

"When will you be ready to do the interview, Mr. Ruby?" Matt asked. Matt was frazzled and beginning to fray at the edges, and he was in no shape to do an interview, but he needed the attention back on real life and not on three boys who didn't exist in his life. The sooner he could get off this island, the better.

"Well, there's no rush now," Ruby said. "Amy needs a couple days of rest and the weather is beautiful. We can spend some time getting to know each other and do some fun things on the island, and then maybe in a few days when Amy is ready, we can do the interview and the photo shoot."

Reynolds was holding her fork, but she wasn't eating. She was staring at Matt and waiting to see what he would say.

"I don't want to intrude, and I'm sorry for almost crashing a plane onto your island, Mr. Ruby."

"Call me Bill."

"I'm a little done in, and I think it best if I head back to New York now. Perhaps we can do the interview at a later date when everyone has..." Matt trailed off. He wasn't sure what to say. Reynolds needed to heal, and then there were the three boys who he did not want to get to know better, and the walls were closing in on him. The panic was back and his hands started to shake. He was a caged animal, and he had to get out of here immediately. "I have an event with my fiancé tomorrow, and I can't miss it," he lied.

Bill smiled, and Matt instinctively knew that Ruby was glad to hear there was no competition in the pursuit of Reynolds. Ruby was fawning over Reynolds, but in a decent way. Of course there was no competition. Matt was engaged, and Reynolds was more like a buddy to him than anything.

"You're engaged?" Ruby asked.

"Yes," Matt said. "But we haven't set a date yet," he added with a smile as he looked at Reynolds. He did this just to get under Ruby's skin, but he saw Reynolds clench her jaw.

"Are you okay, Reynolds?" Matt asked.

"Yes," she said looking down at her plate of food. It's just my neck." Her face was turning red and Matt wasn't sure if she was in pain or embarrassed, and he didn't want to ask. He stood and placed his napkin on the table.

"Will you invite me back for the interview if I go now?" he asked Ruby.

"Of course," the movie star said graciously. "As soon as Amy is ready, we will let you know and you can come over by boat," he said with a chuckle.

"Yes," Matt said, turning to leave and almost stepping right into the bodyguard who he hadn't known was standing behind him. The intimidating figure took two steps backwards and nodded, but his gaze didn't leave Matt's eyes.

"I will show you where to go," Reynolds said.

"Donnelly can do that," Ruby said softly, but she stood.

"It's okay," she said. "I'll just be a minute." Reynolds passed by Matt and he followed her out of the room. She walked him through the maze of hallways and rooms to the front door.

"So, you and Bill Ruby?" Matt questioned. "I didn't see that coming."

"Is it so surprising?" she asked defensively.

"The man is an international movie star and is in every tabloid show and magazine. I'm just amazed I didn't know because usually that stuff is plastered all over."

"Usually the magazines make up a story to have a story, and it was years ago," she told Matt.

He glanced over at Reynolds as they walked, the neck brace keeping her face forward. Her short, curly hair was disheveled and her bangs were bouncing into her eyes as she moved. She was plain, no makeup as usual, but she had a classic look about her. Her nose and her mouth were perfectly dainty, and her chin was pointed at just the right angle. She was actually pretty, Matt noticed.

"Sure, magazines make up stories, but I don't know how they missed this one. Bill Ruby is clearly in love with you. I just can't wrap my mind around it."

"Is it so hard to believe?"

"It's just that, you're nothing like a woman."

"Thanks a lot!" she said as she hit Matt gently in the stomach.

"No, it's not like what you're thinking. It's just that you're not like the goddess type I'm used to seeing on Bill Ruby's arm. You're more like a buddy."

They walked out onto the perfectly manicured gravel drive where a servant was standing next to the open door of a car. Bill

Ruby had clearly watched too much of Downton Abbey. Matt was certain that the moment the car was down the drive, more servants would jump from the bushes to rake the stones back into position.

"If we're such good buddies, Matt, why are you leaving me here with those three boys? We have to figure out what happened today." Reynolds was starting to tear up, and he could see that she also felt that she might be losing her mind.

"I don't know what the hell happened," Matt said, uncomfortable with her insecurity and filled with resentment toward the entire situation. He'd listened intently when Reynolds was telling Bill Ruby what had happened to them. Matt had been relieved to hear that Amy had experienced the same wash of white light, and had felt the same pulling at her skin, and had the same confusion about the appearance of the three boys. Still, he had no intention of sticking around Ruby Island for a few days just to find out he was going crazy. He was not a father, and that was that.

"There was that light and that energy and they were just there," Reynolds said. "Something is happening here, Matt. We need to talk to those boys to find out what they know."

"I only have one interview to do, and that is with Bill Ruby. If you want to stay here to talk to those kids, go right ahead."

"It was the Bermuda Triangle, Matt. I told you we shouldn't fly here."

Matt's neck started to burn with his rising blood pressure. "Reynolds, those are not our children. We left New York this morning together. We landed on Ruby Island today, the same day we left New York. For all I know, Ruby is pumping this island full of hallucinogens just to get a rise out of people."

She took his arm and pleaded with him. "Come on, Matt. It's me. I was with you on that airplane. Something happened. We have to figure out what is going on."

"I'll see you in a few days, Reynolds," Matt said, ducking into the car. The servant closed the door and it began pulling forward.

Matt realized he was sweating all over and he had to gulp back his emotions. Reynolds was the most self-assured person that he had ever known. She always had a plan for any situation that might present itself. It was upsetting to him to see her so vulnerable.

Bill Ruby has a world-class staff to care for her, Matt thought, as he wiped his hands on his pants and tried to forget about Ruby Island.

AMY HAD FORGOTTEN how good life with Bill Ruby could be. His island was truly a tropical paradise, and his staff was wonderful. She knew that he had poached his butler and some of the other staff during his stays at six star hotels around the world. They had all earned their place within Bill's life. They were loyal to Bill's privacy and were always at hand but never intrusive.

Amy had been furious when Matt drove away. She wanted to run away too, but even if her injury would allow it, she couldn't turn away from the three boys who claimed to be her sons. She had never seen them before, and she'd never been pregnant in her life, yet there was something so undeniably familiar about them.

Bill went to watch his movie in the theater with the boys leaving Amy to relax, and it wasn't long before the youngest boy found her. He walked over to the couch and lay down next to Amy, putting his head on her shoulder and snuggling up right next to her. Amy was startled, but it was comfortable, so she lie still. He had a stuffed dinosaur in his hands, and she was now certain that Bill stocked a small toy store on the island.

"Mom?" the boy asked.

"Yes?" Amy said, surprised she had responded.

"Why were they shooting everyone in Bill's movie? I mean, maybe we shouldn't be here with him if he's that kind of person."

Amy's eyes opened wide as she remembered that all of Bill's movies were rated PG-13 or rated R, and she was glad the boy had removed himself from the violence. "That's not Bill in real life. He's acting. He's playing a part. It's his character that is chasing the bad guys."

"So he has bad character?" the boy asked again.

"It's make believe, Benji," Amy said, finally remembering his name.

"So it's all made up, like at home when we would put on plays for each other and pretend to be someone else?" Benji asked.

"Yes, like a play," Amy's voice shook as she answered. "I don't think you should watch any more of Bill's movies. Let's see if there's something on TV you could watch." Amy changed the channels until she found a cartoon.

"What is that?" he asked, but Amy didn't answer. She let him watch and she closed her eyes enjoying his giggles. "Mom, can you put your hand in my hair like usual?" he asked. Amy took a deep breath and started brushing her hands through his long, fine hair until they both fell asleep.

The next day, Bill gave them their space and Amy took the boys to a large beach along the south coast of the island. The water was tropical and the boys were fearless. They swam like champions, even Benji, not afraid of the waves that would tumble upon them. She was able to learn their names and personalities by watching them interact with each other.

She called the oldest William because it was too confusing with two Bill's on the island. He had pulled a long branch from a copse of trees and expertly sharpened it with a stone. He trotted back out into the water and speared a large, red fish, pulling his catch up over his head in triumph. Amy had never fished nor hunted, and she didn't want to watch too closely at how they handled the fish. The boys each took turns with the spear, and before long they had caught ten fish. She watched their long hair move in the breeze, watched how they used their bodies as a tool in the water, and listened to their sharp and confident speech. It was as though they were primitive, yet educated.

A valet brought a chest full of ice down from the truck and the boys spent some time playing with the ice before putting the fish in the cooler. "Can we have more pop?" Steven asked the valet.

"Everything in moderation," William answered, and Amy could hear her own mother in that.

Amy had applied sunscreen three times, but the boys seemed immune to the stinging rays. She had made them put it on when they had first left the house, but their fully tanned frames seemed to beat off the sunburn. *They must get that from Matt's side of the family*, she caught herself thinking and then recoiled.

She had talked to them at length this morning, and they told her about their life on the island, and then repairing the airplane to get off the island so they could get to civilization. She could hear both herself and Matt in the way they talked, and it was all she could do to not burst into tears. She'd excused herself five times to go in the bathroom to cry in private. Yesterday, her mother was encouraging her to get a life. Yesterday, she had an impossible crush on Matt. Yesterday, she left civilization for this island, and today she had a family.

Amy was reconciling herself to the fact that she was the boys' mother, but Matt had run for the hills. And as wonderful as they were, she couldn't allow herself to start thinking of them as a family.

Matt watched the doors open, but he didn't immediately step off the elevator. He had landed on Ruby Island forty-eight hours earlier, and his nerves were still shaken. He hadn't heard from Reynolds and he didn't know if that was good or bad. Good probably. He tried to forget the faces of the three boys as he stepped into the magazine lobby. His phone buzzed in his pocket and he looked at the number. It was the owner of the aircraft looking for him again, but this time Matt wouldn't answer the phone.

He had already told the man that he would get the aircraft back, and that he was just getting aircraft fuel brought over to the little island to refill the tanks. That had worked for a few hours, but it turned out to Matt's chagrin that although the islands were separated by water, the pilots might as well have been sitting in lawn chairs right next to each other and gossiping about the tourists. The pilot had just left him a message that he knew of no request for fuel and that he could put in the request if Matt would give him a different credit card number.

Matt had winced at the message. He had panicked in the Miami airport and had called the credit card company from a payphone and told them he had lost it on his trip. He didn't want the deductible for the airplane put against his credit. He didn't want the FAA to find out what had happened. If he was honest, he still didn't know what had happened.

Matt shook his head and walked toward Nicole. She was smiling at him, but her eyebrows were raised and that was never good. Matt tried to look past her to his father-in-law-to-be's office, but Nicole called out to him. He couldn't ignore her anyway. She was the editor on his Bill Ruby story.

"Matt Cole," she said conclusively, like she was hammering each syllable into the table.

"Hey, Nicole." He tried to smile but his lips got hung up on his dry teeth. He instinctively looked over to her desk calendar and noticed the date and year. It had been two days since he'd rented the airplane, not thirteen years and two days. He smiled with the knowledge that he was right, but he was still a bit frantic and shaken at what had taken place. Although he'd binge watched documentaries in the last two days, Matt would not admit to himself that something had happened to him and Reynolds in the Bermuda Triangle.

"So, Amy decided to stay behind after the interview, eh?" she asked. Matt thought about lying, but he knew that Reynolds was friends with Nicole, so he thought partial truth was better.

"She was injured when we arrived at the island, but don't worry. She's all right. The doctor wanted her to stay for a couple of days. He had her in a neck brace but I think it was just for show. She seemed fine when I left." Matt didn't sit down at first, passing Nicole a few steps and turning his body toward Charley's office as though he had an important meeting he was late for.

"Matt," Nicole clicked reproachfully. "Amy has asked to put off the article for two weeks, so she must be more hurt than she's letting on."

"Really?" Matt asked and backtracked to sit down opposite Nicole.

"She called me and asked for your cell phone number. She said her phone was broken and she was calling from Bill Ruby's house." Nicole was leaning forward and Matt didn't know if she was trying to get information from him, or just dishing out what she knew.

"She did?" he asked and looked at his cell phone dismissively. This was an old cell phone he'd kept in a drawer for three years. He'd had to pull it out when he returned since his phone had also broken in the... well, in whatever that crazy lightning strike was. Matt grimaced. His phone was fried, and he had lost it on the boat ride back to the main island. Actually, it had been swept away by a rogue wave that had almost rolled the boat over. The men on the boat were visibly shaken and shocked, and they had told Matt that a big wave like that had never happened before on calm water. It only happened during a bad storm. Matt Cole was starting to think that Ruby Island hated him. It was a ridiculous thought though. How could an island hate him? Still, the fog and white light, the strange boys, and the rogue wave; his heart rate increased just thinking about it, and he made a silent promise to never return to that place.

"You can call her if you want to. Bill had some spare phones on the island and she was downloading her info from the cloud when I was talking to her." Matt grit his teeth. Of course the perfect Mr. Bill Ruby had spare phones laying around his island. He probably had a cell phone store in his mansion.

He'd had no cell phone, ergo no one's phone number, no email, no internet. It had made an interesting journey to the main island and then the hop back to Miami and connection to New York. He'd been forced to sit and look at the wall or read whatever he could find. It gave Matt a better perspective on his parents and how they could just sit in a room for long periods of time reading or deep in thought, with no need for electronics. Matt wasn't nostalgic about this though, he was angry. Bill Ruby could have just as easily furnished him with a new cell phone.

He looked in his phone for Reynolds' contact information, but there was none. This phone was from before he'd known her. Still, what would he tell Reynolds? He didn't know who those boys were, and he wasn't going to be able to play the part that she wanted him to play. Nicole was staring at him, and Matt forced a smile.

"She was okay, I promise. The doctor said forty-eight hours, and when I left, she was walking around and sitting at the table to eat and everything. She looked okay to me," he said, before choking on his dry throat.

Reynolds wasn't just fine when he had left. She had been trying to convince him to stay and sort out the three children who had been zapped down from a spaceship. Matt had binged on too many YouTube videos about the Bermuda Triangle since he had been back, and he shook his head at his own thoughts.

"Well, you know Amy and Bill go way back," Nicole said, with a wink at Matt. He scratched at his neck and realized that had become a tick he had developed in the last two days, and it usually occurred when he heard Bill Ruby's name. "How is the article coming?"

"I'm not ready to turn in an article yet," he confessed.

"That's okay," Nicole said. Matt knew that it was the editor's job to push for drafts, and she wasn't pushing at all. "Take your time on this one, Matt. If Amy is staying on the island for a while, you might have a new story to write when she comes back. Maybe it will be a story about Bill and Amy." Nicole winked and then watched Matt scratch his neck again, and she thought he had clenched his jaw. He stood and headed toward Charley's office, and she called after him. "Matt, a small island hopper service has been calling looking for you. Did you guys have a problem with your travel?"

"No, no!" Matt said and then caught himself. "I called down because I think I left my tablet on his plane. We flew private the last leg. Bill arranged it," he lied. Matt cursed himself remembering he'd goaded the guy with his business card and the name of the magazine to earn his trust. Of course a huge conglomerate would take care of the aircraft if anything happened, he remembered saying. He would have hit himself in the forehead if his future father-in-law hadn't been staring at him through the huge glass wall that separated them.

Matt smiled at Nicole and pointed toward Charley, and she disapprovingly said "Mmmm hmmmm," loud enough for Matt to hear as he walked away.

"Matt," Charley said before he had even stepped into the office. "How is Amy? She's staying there for two weeks, and she's injured. Why didn't you call me?" Matt could see that Charley was very worried about Reynolds. "What happened? You don't seem concerned." Matt felt as though Charley was accusing him, but he also got the impression Charley was fishing to see how worried Matt was about Reynolds. He read this as a test.

"Reynolds is fine," Matt said confidently. He took a seat and tried to relax. "Nicole tells me that Reynolds used to have a thing with Ruby. That must be the delay. She was just fine when I left."

"Just fine?" Charley asked slowly. Matt tried not to squirm in his seat. His boss wasn't a big man, but he was powerful, and he knew it. Charley didn't stare through people, he stared into them.

"Are you fishing for something specific, Charley?" Matt asked him, nervous that he might have heard about the three boys who had turned up claiming he was their dad. Since Nicole didn't bring it up, Matt thought he was still in the clear. He wasn't so sure now.

"Mr. Robinson," Charley corrected Matt.

Matt cleared his throat. He had called Charley by his first name for a couple of years, but when Sarah had introduced Matt as her boyfriend, all amiability went out the door.

"Maybe I am fishing a little," Charley admitted. "Why is there an aircraft charter service calling for you?"

Matt hesitated and Charley leaned forward. Matt took a deep

breath and sat up in his chair. He exhaled the truth. "It was taking forever to get there and we had to take a hopper from Miami just to get a boat."

Charley nodded. "Go on."

"So, I rented the charter aircraft so we could get to the island quicker. I just wanted to get the interview over with to get back home. I know how much Sarah wanted me back."

"Matt, you're not the first idiot this year to try to fly to Ruby Island, but you might be the last." Charley tossed his phone to Matt where there was a small story about a plane crashing near Ruby Island.

"But we didn't crash. We landed just fine."

"And that's how Amy got hurt? When you landed just fine?"

"I'm telling you, Mr. Robinson, that Reynolds is fine. I just wanted to finish the job and get back to Sarah."

"You wanted to get back so you could explain why you were on a trip to a tropical island with a beautiful girl?" his future father-in-law pressed, and now Matt knew he was being toyed with.

"I was with a girl and almost crash-landed a plane into a trop-ical island, where a dashing, tanned, superstar hero rode up on a motorcycle to rescue us, where said girl is staying to spend some quality time with dashing superhero," Matt quipped sarcastically.

"You sound jealous," Charley said.

"I am. I'll never have abs like Bill Ruby," Matt laughed and then scratched at his neck.

"Mr. Ruby, thank you for finally taking my call," Matt said.

"Come on, Matt, call me Bill. I'm practically an uncle to your boys." Bill was smiling, and he loved the silence that followed. He wouldn't allow himself to be badgered by anyone ever again now that he was Bill Ruby, international superstar. That's why he had waited days to take this call. He wanted Matt to squirm for many reasons. Matt was his ball of yarn this week, and he would toy with him like a cat until he was good and done.

"Did you get my messages?" Matt asked, not wanting to bring up the airplane again, but needing desperately to resolve the issue. He ignored the comment about the boys. Matt had accepted that they were real, just not that he had anything to do with their existence.

"Of course I did, Matt, but I have to do what is best in this matter."

"So, you will return the airplane?" Matt was anxious during the silence that followed and he could practically hear Ruby's smile across the ocean.

"That is in conflict of what would be best in this situation, Matt, and you know that. I don't want anyone to know that you landed safely on the island. I can't have people buzzing the island to get pictures of me and my guests. As far as I'm concerned, the airplane crashed."

"Bill, as I explained to your staff, I'll lose my pilot's license and be investigated if they think I crashed a plane. I need you to call the charter service and tell them that they will get their plane back." Matt was trying to sound firm but not rude. He was glad Bill Ruby wasn't standing in front of him though, because he might have punched him in the face.

"Listen, Matt," Ruby said. The hairs on the back of Matt's neck rose. He'd heard that direct voice before, in the movies, just before Ruby's character was going to threaten his prey. "I know you are a friend of Amy's so I'd like to help you for her sake, but I don't want the plane charter to even know I am involved. I'm well known," he paused and Matt filled in the blanks.

"Mr. Ruby," Matt said more sarcastically than he'd intended. "Bill, help me out here. I was just trying to get the interview completed in a timely manner so that I could get back to New York. I don't want any trouble."

Bill Ruby laughed heartily at this, and Matt shook his head and bit his tongue. It was an impossible situation. Matt wanted to rub shoulders with celebrities. That's the reason he had pursued this job. He wanted to be part of that New York City he'd heard of, the one that glitters and shines. He loved being engaged to Sarah because, well, she was gorgeous, but it also opened doors to events that he wanted to attend. It was about pulling up in a limousine, moving to the front of the line, and having what everyone else wanted.

Matt wanted to forget about Ruby Island and get back to his life here, the life that he had worked so hard to create. It hadn't been easy, though, because the boys' faces kept him up at night, and he wavered between finding out who they really were and never sleeping again.

Ruby's laughter finally tapered off. "Matt, I understand, I really do." He said this in an empathetic tone that made Matt wonder if he'd been reading his thoughts through the phone. "But if you didn't want any trouble, you shouldn't have flown to Ruby Island. I have to contend with the paparazzi and there are already enough rumors about me, Matt. I have to take precautions. Forget about the plane," he said as though he was referring to a rubber ducky. "The plane has already been towed out to sea and sunk."

Matt didn't think he had heard correctly. He cleared his throat and croaked, "What?"

"We sank the plane, Matt. We towed the plane out to sea, took some photos and leaked them to make a good story out of it. I owe you for that." The walls pulled in on Matt and he almost fell over. "Just take the hit on your insurance, and I will wire you the money to pay the deductible on the plane."

"You can't do that," Matt said.

"It's nothing, Matt, really."

Matt realized they were both having a different conversation. If he paid the deductible, then the National Transportation and

Safety Board would be all over him and he might never pilot an aircraft again. "Bill," Matt tried to sound calm but realized it was futile, "I can't let it hit my insurance because then I will lose my pilot's license for crashing an airplane."

"So I will wire you the money to pay for the airplane straight out, and no one has to know."

Matt could hear Ruby calling to someone in the background. It was probably Reynolds lying in a chair beside the pool, while his world came crashing down. It wasn't her fault that he was in this mess. She had warned him not to fly. Why had he been so arrogant? Was he trying to show off? Matt took a deep breath. Figuring out his motives had never been his strong suit.

"I'll have someone call you about the wire transfer, Matt. I've got to go now. It was a pleasure talking to you." After the line went dead, there was neither click nor dial tone like there used to be when he was growing up. There was just utter silence.

CHAPTER 6

"**We** took care of him, Mr. Ruby," Donnelly said as Ruby returned to the patio table.

"Good. Thank you, Mr. Donnelly." There were five plates of fruit decadently arranged at each place setting. Ruby sat next to Amy, but the boys were still splashing around in the pool.

"Am I interrupting?" she asked.

Bill smiled and patted Amy's hand. He loved having her here again, and he would do anything to make her happy. "Nothing of importance. The owner of the airplane that you borrowed was asking around. It seems he never got his plane back." Ruby chuckled as Amy's face turned red. "Don't worry, Amy, it's taken care of. I can't have the locals knowing that an aircraft actually landed on my island."

"I know," she said, but she couldn't help but think of Matt. She had no idea what might happen with the charter service, and she was worried. She mentally chastised herself for caring at all. Matt Cole was a pompous ass who'd flown to Ruby Island against her warnings, he'd dared her to fly with him, and he'd abandoned her with the three boys days ago.

"It's all right, Amy. I've taken care of everything." Bill Ruby's confident smile put Amy at ease, and she took a deep breath and tried to relax. Bill turned his attention to the boys and then nodded at Donnelly. The butler looked out of place calling the boys over for a snack, but they raced each other to the edge and swarmed upon the table like a pack of ravenous dogs getting Amy and Bill wet in their play.

"Have something to eat and let's talk about what we'll do this afternoon," Bill said to the boys with a satisfied smile. They could literally do anything they wanted to, but luckily for Amy, the boys claimed to have been raised on an island with no electricity, no television, no Internet or cell phones, and they were happy to play on the island as it was. Her heart skipped a beat as she looked at the oldest boy, William, and noticed for the tenth time that he looked a lot like Matt. Her concern over the aircraft faded fast as she remembered how quickly he had left them on the island. It was a shocking day, but he had run away like a scared rat.

For her part, she was glad that she had decided to stay on the island to get to know these boys, and she was now convinced that against all odds, she was somehow their mother. There was something so familiar about each of them. They were different in their own ways, but the same too. And the way they were so relaxed with her, no one child could pretend that well with an adult who was a stranger. She had been through that flight in her mind a million times, and she had no explanation for what had happened. Bill said it was the Bermuda Triangle and anything could happen, and as the days went by, Amy was letting go of her doubt.

The boys ate their food in one bite and ran back to the pool, jumping in and causing huge splashes as they landed. Bill laughed out loud, and Amy watched him enjoying himself. "You really like spending time with them," she commented.

"I really do!" Bill told her. "It's like they haven't seen anything in the world, so every time I pull out a gadget, their eyes get wide and they go nuts. Just driving in a car makes them happy. It's fun to watch." Bill stared at the boys and Amy knew that look. He was reflecting on his choices, and he was thinking of what it would be like to be a father. She didn't want to have this conversation with him right now, so she cut his thoughts short.

"What did you boys decide to do this afternoon?" Amy asked.

"We're going over to scale the ravine on the west side of the island."

"Is it safe?"

"For them it is," Bill said. "I've worked with expert climbers, but these boys aren't afraid of anything. They go up a wall like it's as easy as climbing stairs."

Amy watched the boys splashing in the water. They seemed to be expert swimmers too, even little Benji. It was obvious that they had spent all their lives playing outdoors.

"Let's take a walk, Amy." His voice was smooth, but Amy could tell that he wanted to have some privacy, so she slipped her sandals on. Bill stood and pulled Amy's chair away from the table and instructed Donnelly to have the boys ready in thirty minutes.

They walked to a beautiful stone path that took them over a small hill and looked over the ocean. You could see the ocean from anywhere on the island. The flowers around them looked indigenous, and it was a beautiful place to walk. Amy didn't know if the path had been put in this spot for this reason or if Bill had the garden installed, but either way, it always calmed Amy to walk through.

"I had Gary do me a favor. Well, I had him do you a favor." He strolled next to her with his hands clasped behind his back.

"Gary!" Amy laughed. "You mean he knows how to lift a finger?" Bill chuckled at the jibe. Amy knew Gary as a loafing cousin who lived in Bill's L.A. mansion and drove Bill's very expensive fleet of cars. Bill knew Gary as his friend and cousin, his only closest confidant, who would keep every secret of Bill's forever.

"Yes, well, he means well." Bill said, side-stepping the conversation for a moment longer. He really didn't know how to tell Amy what he had done, and he wasn't sure if she would be very pleased with him by the time they made it to the other end of the stone walk.

"Gary goes to a DNA lab about twice a year for me. He presents them with a specimen of hair, and they run it to his DNA on file. The women at the lab think that Gary is quite a player." Bill waited a beat to let this sink in. "Gary pays extra for a rush job, but they don't know that the DNA on file is not Gary's, it's mine." Amy laughed but it was forced. "I don't play around much anymore, Amy, but when you're a celebrity, ladies you never met before come out of the woodwork."

Amy had seen this when she was dating Bill, and she remembered feeling sorry for him. People really do stupid things around celebrities. She figured it was the price they paid for wealth and popularity.

"Amy, I hope you don't mind, but I sent Gary some samples to run for me." Bill waited and he could see that she was starting to work things out on her own. "Would you like the test results?"

Amy stopped walking and put her hands over her face. She was certain that she was somehow related to these boys, even though she couldn't explain it, but to know it for certain with DNA results, that would be more final than she had planned. Still, she would need to have the proof to move forward.

Her hands shook and she felt tears roll down her cheeks, and Amy wasn't sure if she was more terrified to find out she was their mother, or to find out they weren't related at all.

"Tell me," she said without pulling her hands away from her face.

"Okay," Bill said. "Well, I took samples from all three boys, and unfortunately, Gary says that I'm not their father." He smiled at her as she pulled her hands away from her eyes and he had succeeded in lightening up the moment. "Amy, you are their mother." He let the words sink in, and as tears continued to fill her eyes, he pulled her close and let her bury her face in his chest. He could feel her heaving for a moment, and then she took a deep breath.

"I thought we shared everything, Amy, but you never told me you had children with this guy, Matt, when we were dating. It's scandalous." He was joking, but Amy pushed away from him.

"I told you what happened, or that I don't really know what happened, Bill. I think I'm losing my mind." Amy turned away and wiped her face dry with the sleeve of her bathing suit wrap. "Is Matt their father?" she asked.

"I don't know. He left so fast that we don't have any of his DNA."

Amy sighed. That didn't matter right now. What mattered was that she was a mother to three boys, one who was almost a teenager. Her entire life had changed three days ago, but now it was official.

"I'm going to take the boys climbing, Amy. You relax here and process all of this. I've gone through the baby-momma thing a lot of times, and it can really make you rethink your whole future."

"Yes, but you were never the baby-daddy. Right?"

Bill nodded. "You've got me there times three." He smiled the soft smile that brought specks of stars into his eyes, and Amy melted a bit.

WHEN AMY and Bill came back to the pool, the boys were already gone. Amy was sure that Donnelly had whisked them inside to get ready for their hike. She was glad that they weren't there though. She was just taking it all in as Bill had recommended. She had a sense that she was their mother, but now she knew for certain. She went to Bill's suite and lay down on the couch while he got ready for his outing. He sat next to her for a moment and wiped the tears from her eyes. He leaned down and kissed her on the forehead and without a word, he left her with a smile.

Amy cried for a long time for reasons she understood and at times she cried just to cry. She had wanted children, she thought, but she almost never expected it to happen. And here she was the mother of three. When she got herself together, she thought about calling Nicole and Lucy, but she picked up the phone and called her mother instead.

"Hi, Mom," Amy said at the sound of her mother's voice.

"This is Mabel," her mother said.

"Mom, it's Amy."

"Yes, sweetheart. How are you enjoying the island? I expected you back by now." Amy had texted Mabel two days earlier to let her know she was going to be away for a few days and that she was with Bill Ruby. Mabel hadn't replied, but she never replied to texts, and Amy wasn't sure her mom had figured that out yet.

Amy took a deep breath and decided there was no way to really say this. "Mabel," she returned to her mother's name because her mother preferred it. "Something happened on this island, or I should say on the way to the island."

"My God, are you okay? I heard about some fool trying to fly to the island, but I knew it wasn't you. As Bill always likes to say, no one flies to Ruby Island."

"I'm fine," Amy said exasperated. "There was an accident though, Mom... Mabel, something happened." Amy was surprised that she was calling Mabel 'mom' again. She hadn't called her 'mom' since she was eight years old unless she was trying to annoy her. "Are you sitting down?"

"Why would I need to sit down, honey? I've heard it all."

Amy took another deep breath and then plunged in.

"Mabel, you're a grandmother." Amy waited over the silent line and let her mother process this fact. She was sure it wouldn't go over easily. Her mom was aging well but she was not accepting her age gracefully. Amy knew that she wouldn't like to hear the word grandmother. "Did you hear me?"

"I'm not sure I heard you correctly. Did you just say the word 'grandmother' to me?"

"Yes, I did say that. You are a grandmother," Amy said a little impatiently. She needed Mabel right now. She needed the strong, carefree mother that Amy had counted on in the past.

"Did that Bill Ruby have your baby in a test tube when you weren't looking?"

"Mabel."

"What? I always said he was a bit too intense about you. He was like a stalker. And when you left here three days ago, you weren't pregnant, honey."

"He's not a stalker. He's just about the nicest man I know." Amy was pacing now. She hadn't realized that she was going to have to convince her mother.

"Amy, were you in that plane crash? Are you all right?" Amy could hear concern in Mabel's voice, and she stopped pacing.

"There wasn't a plane crash."

"Yes, there was. There were photos on the news of a small plane sinking near Ruby Island. I didn't think anything of it because I know you go there by boat."

Amy wondered what Mabel was talking about since they had landed on the island in one piece, but she got a sinking feeling in her gut that she should hang up and call Matt right away. What if he had been stupid enough to try to fly off the island? He couldn't have though, because if there was anything wrong, Bill would have told her. She took a deep breath and readied herself for the task at hand.

"I was in the plane with Matt Cole from work, and there was a flash of light." Amy told Mabel what had happened from the white haze that had engulfed them to the boys showing up out of nowhere, but she omitted the engine failure and the almost crashing into the sea. When she was done telling her story, there was a minute of silence.

"The Bermuda Triangle. It was the Bermuda Triangle," Mabel said. "Remember Betty Stringer? She was on some charter in the Bahamas and she went through the Bermuda Triangle and her plane had to land on the water. Luckily it had pontoons and she was rescued in less than twenty-four hours."

"Mabel," Amy groaned, although she believed in the Bermuda Triangle whole-heartedly today. "You are a grandmother. I have DNA proof. I will explain more when I see you."

There was silence on the line, and then Amy heard a small exhale.

"Mabel?" she asked.

"I'm here, sweetheart." Amy could hear tears in her mom's voice, but her mother never cried. She was a rock, the captain of the ship, and she always kept it together. Amy assumed she was having a hard time with the word 'grandmother'.

"Come on, Mabel. It's not like the doctor just diagnosed you with cancer."

"Bite your tongue, Amy. It's not about me. I'm just so happy for you."

This took Amy aback. Her mother was not known to show emotion, and Amy could feel her sincerity through the phone. "Thank you, Mom. We're going to stay down here for a few more days. It's quite a shock, and we need time to get to know each other before I come back to New York. Bill is taking care of everything."

"Of course he is. That's what Bill does," Mabel said with a touch less sarcasm this time.

AMY LAY in the king-sized white bed with Benjamin, her youngest son. Steven, the middle boy, was asleep on the floor.

She found herself relishing the simple sound of their breathing and smiled a half-smile. It was all too unreal, but it felt right to her in some way.

There was a light knock on the door and Bill Ruby peeked his head inside. He looked at Amy and the boys and smiled his million-dollar smile, and Amy felt that old familiar surge of happiness she felt when she was around him. She had always been attracted to Bill. A woman would have to be dead not to be dazzled by him. Even now in his khaki shorts and white unbuttoned shirt, his skin tanned golden all the way down past his belly button, he was casually irresistible.

"William likes having his own room," Bill whispered.

"When the boys said we all lived together, I didn't realize they meant in the same room," Amy whispered back.

Bill came to the side of the bed and held his hand out in question, and Amy nodded. He pulled the covers back and lie down right next to Amy. She picked her head up and he put his arm around her, and it was all so familiar.

"I've missed sleeping with you," Bill said, and Amy hit his arm lightly.

"Bill," she warned.

"What? You are the only girl I ever slept with that I didn't sleep with."

"Yeah," Amy said. She put her hand up to her face. As much as Bill dazzled her and made her feel comfortable, it was moments like this that Amy felt exposed as a fraud. She never considered herself beautiful, and she couldn't understand what someone like Bill Ruby could possibly see in her. They were great friends and she wished she could get over it, but there was always that soft voice reminding her that she wasn't completely comfortable with him on every level. Sure, she was comfortable in his arms and he'd always been completely respectable, but the spark just wasn't there for Amy.

"I've been trying to figure out what's going on. What am I supposed to do? I don't even know how old I am now. Ugh."

Bill chuckled and kissed Amy on the forehead. "You're the same age you were a week ago."

"So you believe me?" she asked.

"Of course, look at these boys. It's all too real to be made up. I mean, they never saw my movies, Amy. They had to be stranded on an island or living under a rock."

"Well at least they knew who you were," Amy said, snuggling into Bill.

"Thank you for naming your first born son, whom you had with another man, after me. Remind me to thank you for that over and over."

"I will remind you on William's birthday every year. Oh my gosh, I don't even know when my son's birthdays are," Amy complained.

"We'll ask them," Bill said, squeezing her shoulder. "And if they don't know, we'll let them choose dates." They talked quietly, and somewhere in the night, the lull of the ocean sang them to sleep.

att's cell phone rang but he didn't answer. He wasn't answering any calls from numbers that he didn't recognize right now. He got a text shortly after the phone rang.

"This is Amy. I just wanted to make sure you're okay. I heard there was a plane crash near Ruby Island".

He texted back, "I'm okay," but left it at that. He was walking into his fiancé's television studio in New York City's Times Square. He loved to watch her under the lights reading the news from a teleprompter. She was great at ad-libbing, and between that and her perfect body, she was a shoe-in for the job. She wasn't a reporter, she was more important than that. Sarah Robinson was a celebrity, and Matt loved to walk into a room with her on his arm.

It wasn't that he liked to see the other men ogling Sarah. He'd heard a song about that: the singer enjoying other guys' reactions to his girl because he knew she was all that. Matt knew that was just a song to get the ladies. No man liked the ogling of his girl. Matt attributed this fact to the primal male instinct to keep what is his. Like male animals fighting in the wild: he'd almost hit a few guys whom he noticed undressing Sarah with their eyes.

Sarah finished her prep work at the news desk and then stood up, her thin figure beautiful under the bright stage lights. Her eyes scoped the studio, and when she saw Matt, her smile lit the room. She moved around the desk and Matt moved to greet her.

"Sarah, you look beautiful as always." Sarah leaned in and rubbed up against Matt. *She's magnificent*, he thought. She was really the whole package: beauty, brains, success. She would take the world by storm, and he would be right there with her.

Matt admired the way Sarah always knew what she wanted without hesitation. She knew what to order on a menu within ten seconds, she knew which moves to make in her career, which apartment to rent, and which parties to attend. He was floundering a bit in life with his current writer's block, but he felt successful when he was with her.

The hair on the back of his neck prickled and he leaned in for a kiss, but she kissed the air next to his cheek.

"I'm on in twenty minutes, babe. Don't mess with the make-up." Matt took a deep breath and smiled, but he was a bit annoyed. She never let him kiss her in public, and no matter where they were, it was always about the makeup.

One of the suits from upstairs came toward them, and Sarah took a step back. "Jim, so nice of you to come down," Sarah gushed to the suit. He took her hand but didn't quite shake it, just holding it out in front of her for a moment too long.

"I need to keep tabs on my new superstar." The suit forgot that Matt was standing there and smiled at Sarah, making sure to check out her figure in the process.

"Jim, have you met Matt?"

"I don't believe I have." The suit turned halfway toward Matt and absently shook his hand.

Matt was about to introduce himself as Sarah's fiancé, but she snapped to attention and barked, "Matt, get me a drink."

"Sure," Matt said, feeling put off. "Coffee?" he asked.

Sarah looked at Matt with the eyes of a disapproving school-teacher. "Matt, I go on in twenty, you know I can't drink coffee right now. Be a dear and get me a bottle of water with a straw."

As Matt walked away, he realized that he was annoyed with the way Sarah had just barked at him. He used to jump at any request, but today he was bothered by her attitude. He chalked it up to his increasing level of stress due to the Ruby Island incident. That's what he was calling it: The Ruby Island Incident. It sounded so sinister, and it was to him. He didn't want to think about it, so he walked faster to get Sarah her water.

He would get her whatever she wanted. They were a couple, a team. What she needed, he needed. He turned back to see Sarah leaning in and touching the suit's arm, and the guy was buying every ounce of charm she was selling. This had never really bothered Matt before, and he shook his head when the word 'bitch' passed through it.

AMY STEPPED out into the hot sun and let it warm her to the core. She was wearing a bikini under her long, white bathing suit wrap. Her pale freckled skin was starting to tan, and she was calm and refreshed. She held the cell phone to her ear and waited for Matt to pick up, but it went to voicemail for the tenth day in a row. She knew he didn't crash the airplane trying to leave the island because he had texted her back once. Still, she wanted to talk to him. She wanted to hear his voice to know that she wasn't losing her mind. He was the only other person on that airplane, and she felt like she needed to at least touch base with him. Of course, there was also the matter of the DNA results. She had officially been a mom for two weeks.

"You look wonderful, Amy," Bill said as he walked past her to the waiting Jeep. He was carrying her camera bag and a cooler. It was strange to see him carrying bags on his own. It wasn't that he was a prima donna, but he paid his staff well to handle things before he even knew what those things might be, and they worked like a well-oiled machine.

Bill was changing, and Amy thought it must have been the time he was spending with the boys. It was like he was a family man all of a sudden, and that had surprised Amy. She watched his gorgeous body load the items and realized she was crazy for thinking of Matt when a specimen like Bill was within arm's reach.

Bill didn't stop to talk to Amy, instead returning to the house to make sure all was ready. They were going on a picnic in a spot the boys had found yesterday. Bill assured Amy that it was a spot that was easy enough to get to, but she slipped on some hiking shoes and carried her flip-flops to the Jeep. She put them in the outside pocket of the bag Bill had placed in her seat. The bag wasn't hers from New York. It was a new bag with a new camera and new film for her to use. He had sent for it two days ago when she had opened her gig bag and realized that all of her film had been used up. She had been shocked to see roll after roll fully used, and even more shocked to see there was wear on the labeling, and the boxes looked faded. There was even a little sand in the bottom of her bag, and she had hastily shaken it out to preserve the film. She had decided to use the new camera because she wanted to have hers properly serviced when they returned to New York.

They, she thought. When *they* returned to New York. It wasn't just Amy anymore, and it would never be again. Those were her boys, her three sons. They knew everything about her, and she could remember nothing. They had reminded Amy that she had used up all the film on the island, taking a photo of the family every once in a while until the film was used up. That was when Bill said he was going to install a dark room for her to develop the film, but Amy said it could wait until she returned home. She didn't tell Bill, but she was terrified to develop that film. She was petrified to see what her life might have looked like together with Matt.

When Bill returned, the two younger boys came running out behind him and piled into the Jeep. Amy noticed that the eldest boy, William, walked to the SUV a bit slower. Amy had come to calling him William since that was his proper name. Her son preferred Bill, but it was just too confusing with Bill Ruby and Bill at the same table. Of course, Ruby joked that she could call him 'Sweetie' like she used to. Amy could see this hadn't gone over good with William, and when he started talking about Matt every five minutes, she realized that to these boys, Matt was their father, and the only man they had seen their mother with. Heck, he was the only man they had seen period.

As the days went by with Bill, Amy could see William and even Steven trusting him less. They liked him when they had his attention, but when it switched to their mother, Amy saw them clam up. She knew it was because of her. The oldest, William, had asked her where their dad went. He reminded Amy of Matt every chance he got, as though she were forgetting.

Of course, he couldn't know that every other thought in her head was about Matt. She was trying to keep it together, trying to move forward as a single mom as Bill put it. She could easily read what Bill wanted, but she wasn't at the point in her life to entertain thoughts of them being a couple again. She would wait on the island until it was time, and then she would return to New York City with the boys and see what kind of life she could put together for them as a family.

Bill stopped at Amy's door and Amy climbed into the passenger seat and tucked the photo bag at her feet. Bill closed the door and walked around the front of the Jeep, his perfect smile melting Amy's confused heart for a moment. Benji scampered around after him and hopped in the front seat on Bill's lap and pretended to drive the SUV. When William finally climbed in the back, Bill actually started the engine and let Benji steer down the main driveway. Benji was a young child, and he enjoyed all of the attention and adventure. Bill was showing the boys a new world, her world. It was a world with houses and cars, swimming pools and electronics, and a world with interesting people and not just their family. Amy frowned at that thought.

This was all new to her, but it was also new to them. They needed to learn about society and the excitement of city life, but they were also sadly entering a time in their lives when their parents were no longer together. That would be much easier for her to accept since she couldn't remember ever being with Matt. It was ridiculous really. She'd had a crush on him for a long time, and they'd never even kissed, not in this lifetime anyway. And yet chances were that her three sons were also his three sons. Whatever stupid little crush she'd had on Matt was that of a little girl. She was a mom now.

Amy put her arm up on the door and twirled her bangs in her fingertips. She absent-mindedly watched the beautiful scenery go by. She laughed to herself that she must have been on a tropical island for the past twelve years to not be taking in the beautiful view each moment, but there were too many thoughts in her mind to contend with. She hadn't allowed the boys to go on the Internet yet, but she knew she would soon. She couldn't take three naive boys to New York City.

The Jeep stopped and Benji climbed over the seat and sat in the back between his brothers. "Uncle Bill," Steven cried, "I want a turn."

Bill laughed with all of the easiness of a gorgeous movie star who was truly enjoying life to the fullest. "You're too big to sit on my lap, Steven. How about I give you some driving lessons on the driveway tomorrow and you can sit here on your own."

"Yes!" Steven yelled behind Amy. She looked at Bill, and he was already looking over to her for permission since she was the mom, but she simply smiled and shrugged.

"Well, we are on Ruby Island."

Bill laughed and reached over to grab Amy's hand, but then he thought better of it and put his hand on the stick shift. Amy had noticed the move, and it bothered her a little. Bill Ruby always did what he wanted, and now he was altering his behavior to please her children. William was sometimes sarcastic when telling certain stories from the island when Bill's name had been brought up, and Amy could hear Matt's influence in his voice. She could see that Bill noticed the change in William too, and it wasn't just her affection he wanted.

She had stayed up for a few hours with William after the other boys had gone to bed on the first night after Matt had left. William had told her and Bill, and Donnelly who was on hand to serve, but really wanted to hear the story first hand, about their adventure. After years of being stranded on the island, they had fixed the airplane as best as they could and chanced trying to find their way back to civilization. Matt and Amy had decided that since William was going to be a teenager soon, this life was not going to be enough for the boys. They would get back to civilization if they could.

The bouncing Jeep jerked Amy back to reality when Bill turned off the dirt road. She turned around and looked at the boys, trying to feign a smile. "Where are you taking me?" she asked as though she was a bit afraid. That made the boys smile back at her.

"You'll have to wait and see, Mom!" Benji called, giggling with the secret. They drove under the tree cover into a small rainforest area on the island. Amy had never been back here before, and when she commented to Bill, he laughed.

"I've been this far in," he said, pointing at the tire tracks that flattened the underbrush, "but I'm not even as adventurous as your boys." She knew what he meant when he came to a stop where the trees thickened and the car track stopped. He turned off the engine and the boys jumped out.

"Come on, Mom!" William called, leading the boys. Amy threw her pack over her shoulder and was glad that she had opted for the hiking boots.

"William, we came out over here yesterday," Bill said.

"I know," William told him. They were the same height, Amy realized as they talked it out. "It's quicker this way though."

"How do you know? You've only been here once," Bill asked.

"I can just tell. Trust me. I understand the terrain."

"Lead on, William." Bill put his hand out and the boys moved into the trees, with Bill and Amy close behind. Bill turned back to Amy and smiled with respect and with a small amount of regret, she thought. "They are really smart, Amy. You must be proud."

And she was.

THEY HAD FOLLOWED William up to a bluff and rested for a moment before descending the other side and navigating around rock formations in the forest. Amy could hear the hiss of water, and at that moment, the boys darted ahead. She watched them scamper easily where she and Bill faltered over fallen branches and around massive tree roots. They looked back a few times, but Bill waved them ahead.

"Don't jump until we get there!" he called.

"Don't jump?" Amy asked.

"You'll see."

The waterfall was along a drop in the forest that was surrounded by trees. Bill had brought Amy around the bottom, and her camera was out of her bag before she had time to take in the whole view. She lifted it to her face for an overview of the shots she would want to take, and then she noticed the boys standing at the top, their shirts already shed.

"Mom, watch!" William called, and before Amy could react, he pulled his arms back and leapt into the air. Amy's heart stopped as she watched him plunge down into the pool at the bottom. She ran forward and a second later William's head popped out of the water.

"Hurry up, William," Steven called from the top.

"Wait a minute," Amy protested, looking into the pool and noticing how shallow the stream coming out of it was. William pulled himself up on the rock and before his feet were out of the water, Steven jumped.

"Cannonball!" he yelled, although he kept his body straight and rocketed into the water as stiff as a board.

"It's okay, Mom. We did this like a thousand times yesterday." William ran past Amy and made for the top while Benji looked over the edge for a minute. Amy pulled her camera up to her eye to zoom in and try to see Benji's face. His hesitation made her assume that he was afraid, but when she looked closely, she could tell that he wasn't scared. He was being meticulous about his jump. After spending two weeks with him, she knew that he was just being Benji. He was more methodical than the other two boys. She clicked a shot of him, and then another, and before she knew it, Benji had jumped over the edge and Amy was capturing it all on film.

"Take a picture of me too, Mom," Steven called as he ran past her to climb to the top.

Bill offered to take Amy to the top, but she said that she'd better do that last today, or she might make the boys stop jumping. She tried to guess the height and realized that it was probably the same height as an olympic diving platform, and she knew there was little chance she would try to jump.

Bill joined the boys and jumped many times himself. He told Amy that he had watched the boys for a long time before trying it. She had grinned at that, knowing that Bill was a daredevil and would typically jump right in. This was a very vertical jump into a small pool opening, and she could understand his hesitation. Amy took several shots of Bill, watching him with the boys through her long photo lens. He was natural with them, and she felt a pang knowing he would be a great father someday.

They ate a lunch of sandwiches and fruit and then the boys played, climbing trees one higher than the next. Amy relaxed on the blanket and breathed in the island air. She had always loved Ruby Island, and she loved Bill Ruby too, but she knew it wasn't romantic love anymore. She wondered if he had read her mind because at that moment Bill returned to the blanket and sat down very close to her. He squeezed Amy's shoulders which always sent shivers over her body. She enjoyed the moment until she could feel Bill's hands soften their pull on her muscles. She knew him so well, and she wished she could say yes to whatever he was about to say, but she wouldn't.

"I can take care of you and the boys, Amy." He moved to face her, but Amy kept her gaze high up in the trees on her three sons. "It's not just the means, Amy. I can really take care of you. You know I love you, and I can't help but love those boys. They were made for an island like this."

Amy smiled and swallowed fast. She didn't expect a declaration like that, and although they had parted ways in the past, she knew that Bill was sincere.

"I thank you for that, Bill, but I need to take the boys back to New York with me." She saw the immediate regret on his face.

"How is it that you can turn me down so easily?" he asked with a gentle smile. Amy knew that not many people ever turned Bill Ruby down in business or pleasure.

"It's not easy, Bill. I'm just too confused to think straight. You're the only friend in the world who could have gotten me through this, and I promise we will come back if things get too weird in New York." Bill smiled and wiggled his eyebrows and Amy shook her head. "We'll come back to visit, Bill."

"I know," he said, obviously hurt by Amy's rejection. He smiled at her and shrugged. "What can I say? I've missed our time together. You're about the only person who talks to me and not movie star Bill Ruby."

"You can call me any time, you know!" Amy said and tossed a napkin in his face. They both laughed and Bill returned to the trees with the boys to enjoy their last afternoon together.

CHAPTER 8

The boys had truly loved the boat ride to Eleuthera island, and it had taken an hour longer than usual because Bill insisted on teaching each of them how to drive the boat and then gave them turns at the wheel. He wasn't showing off for them, Amy knew. He was truly enjoying their company as much as they were enjoying his. Amy sometimes forgot that everything was new to the boys, and each leg of the trip seemed to take extra time because they asked hundreds of questions about what things were and how they worked. She could tell that they'd had some education on the island because they could all read words and numbers, and she felt some pride knowing that it was she or Matt who had taken the time to teach them to read. She wondered how they had done it while stranded on the island with no books.

Bill tried to accompany them back to New York, but Amy insisted that she go back without him, although she didn't say no when he offered his private jet to her. Benji had sat next to Amy the entire flight, and she held his hand and stroked his hair. He had flown once in his life, and that time the plane had almost crashed. Amy could see that Benji was not going to forget that any time soon.

The older boys had spent some of the flight sleeping, and she woke them when they were approaching New York City. They looked out the window at the sprawl of houses and were excited to see the skyline. Amy tried to warn them how crowded the city would feel after the solitude of the island, but that just excited them more. They had been watching movies and television shows on the island and had seen Hollywood's version of the real world. The glitter and glamour had excited them, and they were ready to plunge in.

There was a limousine waiting on the tarmac when they landed, and Amy was grateful because she wasn't sure she could handle the boys and their luggage on her own. The boys were arriving in New York City for the first time, and in some ways so was Amy. She typically traveled light and unfettered, and that time in her life had come to a sudden stop. As the limo made it's way from Teterboro Airport in New Jersey to her mother's Upper West Side brownstone, the boys' faces were glued to the windows as they took in the traffic, the buildings, and people of New York City. Amy felt a pang of panic rising in her stomach, and she wasn't sure if it was concern for her sons in the city, or the fact that in thirty minutes, she and the boys would come face to face with Mabel.

When the limousine stopped in front of the house, the front door of the brownstone was flung open and Amy saw Mabel waiting at the top of the stairs dressed up in a full powder blue skirt and jacket with cap and half veil pulled down. She remembered her mom doing that the first time Amy brought Bill Ruby to meet her, but that was the only other time Mabel bothered to come out and greet Amy or a guest.

Amy left the limousine and felt tears welling in her eyes, but she didn't know why. She knew that the reality of being home was hitting her, and she slowly took the stairs one by one and hugged Mabel. She was crying now, and she didn't know how this feeling of missing her mom had manifested because she had only been gone for two weeks.

"Bring the bags inside," Mabel called to the limo driver who nodded. "Come in," Mabel said to Amy and the boys. She turned and swept into the house leaving Amy to wipe her tears. Amy didn't want the boys to see her crying again. They had caught her a few times on the island when she was afraid she was having a mental breakdown. If it weren't for the DNA test, she might have checked herself into a mental health facility. Amy wiped the tears on her sleeve and turned sideways in the entrance, showing the boys to the front room of the house.

Amy was going to introduce the boys, but the driver entered with the first round of bags and looked at Mabel who nodded. He left them in the large foyer and turned to get the rest. "Young man," Mabel said to the forty-something driver. "I will need your services in thirty minutes. Mr. Ruby won't mind keeping you on for the day." Mabel smiled, and the man agreed with a nod and a smile before going out.

"Mabel," Amy muttered. She knew that Bill wouldn't mind paying for the limo for the day, and she also knew her mom's penchant for enjoying Bill's wealth from the sidelines. She shook her head but didn't argue the point.

"Mabel, I would like to introduce you to your grandsons." Amy watched her mom step in next to her and click her heels. She had a warm smile on her face, and Amy thought she saw the crack of emotion from the way her mom's lips were quivering, so she looked away or they might both be crying in a minute. "Boys, this is your grandmother."

"Grandmother," they said tentatively, but Benji moved in and gave Mabel a hug.

"Call me Mabel," she said. "I'm too young to be a grandmoth-er." Mabel winked at Amy who rolled her eyes.

"That's Benjamin, but we call him Benji," Amy said.

"Hello, Benji," Mabel said as she hugged Benji and scruffed his hair.

"This is William," Amy said as the eldest stepped forward. He too hugged Mabel, which surprised Amy, but her mom gently returned the hug and put her hand on top of William's head to scruff his hair too. She pushed him away and took a good, long look. "You are very handsome, William."

"Thank you," he said, and stepped aside.

"I understand you go by Bill for short," Mabel said slyly, and Amy bit her lip. "Your mother tells me you were named for Bill Ruby. Isn't that ironic?" Mabel looked at Amy who began to sweat. She didn't like telling her mom that little tidbit on the phone, and she knew this wasn't the last she'd hear of it.

"Bill Ruby is a great guy, but I go by William now." He tried to sound grown up when he said this. "I was Bill on the island where I grew up, but I'm older now, and I would like to be called William." Amy could hear Bill Ruby's fortitude in William's tone, and she knew he had made a great impression on all of the boys.

"Well, it's nice to meet you, William," Mabel said graciously.

"And this is Steven, who must be named after Dad," Amy said with a flicker of regret in her voice. She missed her father immensely, and the way Mabel nodded without a word told Amy that her mother missed him too.

He was a steady husband and father, a reasonable and well-respected man, and he loved Mabel and Amy to a fault. In a world of people searching for purpose, he knew that his purpose was to love 'his girls' and to take care of them. He'd told Amy that her whole life, and she wondered how he'd managed to figure that out when others struggled. She looked at her own boys and could for the first time see what he'd meant. Amy had aspirations in photography, but her lens was shifting. Her purpose was to get to know her boys and to figure out a way for them to grow up in a world they knew nothing about.

Steven waved at Mabel and smiled with a hint of suspicion.

Amy had seen his reserve at times on Ruby Island, and she knew he would warm up to Mabel in time.

Mabel was flamboyant but typically reserved with affection, and she winked at Steven, and then leaned forward and mussed his hair with her fingers as she had done to the other boys. "No hugs for now," Mabel said.

The chauffeur had the last load of luggage in the foyer, and he tipped his cap at Mabel. "We will be out shortly," she told him. Amy looked around the room and then at the pile of bags they had acquired from Bill who had ended up furnishing a wardrobe for each of the boys.

Amy said, "Don't worry, Mabel. We'll find somewhere to go. It's too small here, and I know you wanted me to move out and find my way." Amy tried to keep any sarcasm from her voice. Her mom had nudged Amy to date and tried to convince her to move out, but Amy didn't like to live alone. She was lonely and allowed herself too many hours of television when she lived alone. She didn't like to use the word depressed, but she knew what it meant.

"Nonsense. You will stay here! I need to get to know these young men." Mabel leaned down and took Benji's hands in hers. "Now, you have grown up on an island, is that right?"

"Yes."

"Have you had ice cream yet?"

"We had some called 'Skinny Cream' on the island with Uncle Bill," Steven said.

"Oh, no! That won't do!" Mabel said with enthusiasm. She took Benji's hand and led him through the high archway at the back of the room. "Come in the kitchen and let me introduce you to Haagen-Dazs," she said over her shoulder with a wink to Amy.

AMY SAT on the couch and put her face in her hands. She was

grateful to her mother for distracting the boys. She didn't think the trip from Ruby Island would take such a toll on her, never mind the easy travel on a private jet followed by door to door limousine service. Amy had been questioning her entire future for two weeks, and returning home brought everything to the surface.

She needed to talk to Matt, but she hesitated trying to call him again. He hadn't answered the phone for two weeks, and he didn't want to talk to the boys. He was in denial, Amy thought. She had accepted the boys before the DNA test proved that she was their mother, and she hoped that Matt might see the light if his test proved the same.

"If you're tired, you should go lie down," Mabel said from the door. She was carrying a small tea cup with a small scoop of Chocolate Chocolate Chip ice cream in it. Amy would have preferred the entire pint, but she knew that Mabel would disapprove of the excess.

"Thanks," Amy said, taking the cup and savoring the first bite.

"You don't have to keep us here, Mabel. I can figure something out."

"I'm sure Bill would put you up at the Four Seasons if you'd like," Mabel answered with a smile. "But just in case not, I had a twin bed installed in your dark room to make more space, and I cleared out my boudoir and had a twin bed installed in there."

Mabel said this with a casual tone, but Amy's jaw dropped. Her mother had kept the fourth bedroom as a private closet and sitting room for the last two decades. Amy always thought it was decadent, but her mother was an uncommon woman.

Amy cleared her throat and took another bite of ice cream. "I guess you really do want us to stay."

"Well then, it's settled," Mabel said. She patted Amy on the knee. "Why don't you decide where you want the boys to sleep while I take them toy shopping. They've never seen a toy store!" Mabel laughed with excitement.

"They've never seen toys," Amy corrected her.

"Well, they are going to have fun with their... Mabel," she stuttered and Amy smiled. "Come, boys, we are going to see New York!"

"Take it easy," Amy said.

"I'll just take them to the toy store," Mabel said with a wink.

"Okay, but they've never been to a city, they don't have cell phones, and if they get lost, they will be really lost."

"What? Uncle Bill didn't get them cell phones?" Mabel wisecracked. The boys each went to Amy to give her a kiss on the cheek, a ritual she was really enjoying. William had told her that it was because Dad had always told them to give their mother a kiss. Since Matt wasn't even answering the phone, Amy decided to give herself the credit for their good manners.

The front door closed, and Amy was alone for the first time in a week. On the island, the only place she was alone was in the bathroom. It seems small children require much attention, and Benji was a bit sad since Matt was gone, so he'd clung to Amy like she might disappear at any moment.

Amy walked to the kitchen and put her cup in the sink, deciding she should get the boys unpacked and straightened out in their quarters. She went in the dark room first and saw the twin bed, but she knew she would have to move it out, not wanting the boys around any chemicals.

She moved her hands along the rows of photos she'd left hanging to dry before she'd left, and it felt like a lifetime ago. Amy felt a burst of spirit and decided not to stall any longer. She would develop the film that was in her gig bag. It was the film she had no memory of using. She had been stalling when Bill offered to set up a dark room on the island because she didn't want to see the images. Amy wasn't sure what she hoped to see in those photos from her thirteen years of lost time.

AMY WOKE on the twin bed in the dark room and rubbed the sleep from her eyes. She'd been in a coma, she thought. She wondered how the bed had ended up in this room, and then she saw the first of the photos hanging next to her, and it all came back.

Well, the actual memory of the image in the photo didn't return, but the hours she spent developing the photos pored over her again, and Amy rolled over and covered her eyes.

She could see what had happened on the island now, and it was just as William had said. They'd crashed, and Amy had photos of the airplane with minor damage. They'd been stranded for a long time, and Amy had seen all of the evidence she needed that the boys were theirs.

There were photos of Amy pregnant and holding the baby, and there were photos of her and Matt in an embrace, close and kissing. There were a lot of pictures of William growing up, and then less of Steven and only a few of Benji because they had been running out of film.

Amy rolled over and looked at the images again. She knew the boys were hers, she'd felt it all along. And as much as she didn't want to admit she'd had a crush on Matt, she knew she was already half in love with him before they had even gotten on that plane. The thing that bothered her now though, was the fact that she could see the proof, and she still couldn't remember a thing.

"The Bermuda Triangle," Amy said to herself. She stood up and left the room, turning the sign on the door to "Enter". Amy could smell the coffee, and she shuffled to the kitchen where she saw Mabel cooking eggs for the boys.

"Mom!" Benji yelled, and he ran over to hug her.

"You left the sign on "Stay out"," Mabel commented. "So we stayed out."

"I'm sorry," Amy said, patting Steven on the head while still holding on to Benji. "I fell asleep on the bed you put in there."

"So it worked out after all," Mabel said, pleased with herself.

Just then the doorbell rang and everyone stopped and looked into the hallway where the sound had come from. Amy noticed the serious looks on the boy's faces, and she smiled at them.

"That's a doorbell, boys. When someone comes to the front door, they push it to announce themselves.

The boys all ran down the hall followed by Mabel who was chiding them to never answer the door to a stranger. Amy shuffled over to get a cup of coffee and she heard a commotion, and then the doorbell rang about fifteen more times, and she knew it was the boys inspecting the newest gadget.

"Mom, it's Uncle Bill!" Amy heard Benji call, and Amy groaned.

"Mabel, wonderful to see you again."

"Bill," Mabel replied. Amy stood in the doorway as Bill crossed the room to kiss Mabel's hand.

"What have you done with my daughter?"

"I cloned her, Mabel. I kept the original," Bill joked.

"Well, keep her, I like this one. She comes with babies," Mabel said, and she patted Benji on the head.

"Mom," Amy complained.

"I told you never to call me that," Mabel retorted, and Bill, William, and Steven all laughed.

Amy's eyes darted to Bill, and he put his arms up and shook his head. "I didn't clone you," he said, as though that was something that deemed an explanation. Amy bit her lip and looked at her boys who were still smiling.

"You think that's funny, boys?" Amy asked William and Steven.

"She's just like you described on the island, Mom," William explained, and Amy's heart sank a little. The island, where they had been a happy family, only she couldn't remember. She loved the boys, but now that she'd seen the pictures, she hated the island. Amy's face turned sour, and so William kept explaining.

"You told us that she didn't let you call her mom, and it's exactly how you would tell it."

"Oh?" Mabel asked. "Do tell."

William turned to his grandmother and Amy moaned. "She acted it out just like that, Auntie Mabel."

"Auntie!" Amy belted, and Mabel waved her off.

"She said you were sometimes eccentric..."

"What is that anyway?" Steven asked. "She looks fine to me."

William punched Steven in the arm and continued. "But she said you were wonderfully understanding, and you always knew just the right thing to do at all times. And she was right, Auntie Mabel." William smiled, and he and Steven joined Mabel and Benji for a group hug.

"You're hugging them?" Amy complained. She couldn't remember the last time her mom had hugged her. Her mom "air hugged" her sometimes, like those passing double cheeked kisses that celebrities did. The boys surrounded Mabel, and they were in an outright embrace.

Mabel shrugged. "Well if you wanted a hug, you should have taken them to the toy store."

"She has a point," Bill said, and Amy glared at him.

"Long time, no see," Amy said, turning to Bill. He crossed the room and embraced Amy, and she took a deep breath and hugged him back. She'd felt beaten up, by herself of course, since she'd seen the photos.

There was really nothing in the world that a hug from Bill couldn't fix. Amy stepped back, still a bit angry and surprised that Bill's hug hadn't cured her this time.

"What are you doing here?" she asked.

"I know you need some space to figure things out, Amy. That's why I sent you ahead without me. But I do have business in the city, and I figured you were under so much pressure, I didn't want to bother you with it." Bill shrugged, and she could see the sheepish side of him emerging. Amy gulped.

"Go on."

"Would you come with me to the Ireland Funds Annual New

York Gala?" Bill cocked his head and smiled. Amy felt a jolt of happy, and she surprised herself by immediately accepting the offer.

"Yes!" she said. "Only if I get to sit next to Liam again." Bill Ruby and Liam Neeson had been friends since their hit movie *Shadow of a Doubt*, and Amy had done the Vanity Fair Magazine photo shoot where she had met both of the men. Liam was, well, Liam Neeson, and Amy was star-struck, and Bill was the new star on the block at the time. He was cocky, and Liam was wise, and they really got along together. It was all Amy could do to get a shot of the two without mischievous grins on their faces.

Amy had attended the Gala a few years ago with Bill, and she'd had a hilarious evening at the table where these men of constant wit ripped each other to shreds.

"I'll have to ask Liam," Bill said with a smile. "You really hurt his pride last time."

Amy had had a bit too much champagne, and according to Bill, she'd said something to Liam in jest that had stumped him. She wasn't surprised. Amy had been raised by Mabel and she loved a good battle of wits. She knew Bill was joking now, but she wished she could remember what she'd said.

"Liam Neeson loves me," Amy said in jest.

"Well then, you are definitely not sitting next to him." Bill smiled.

"Go," Mabel called from the next room. "I can keep an eye on the boys."

"When is it?" Amy asked, her face crunching up, hoping he wouldn't say tomorrow.

"It's on Thursday night," Bill said.

"And what is today?" Amy asked. Her ordeal had made knowing the day of the week a futile need.

"It's Wednesday," Bill said. "Can Cindy bring over some things for you to try on this afternoon?"

"Of course she can," Mabel said, entering the room. "Remind me to Cindy, too."

"Yes, ma'am," Bill said, smiling at Mabel's squint toward him.

"Trish will be here Thursday at five to get you ready," he told Amy, kissing her on the cheek. Amy knew from their previous days dating that Bill retained a couple of stylists in a couple of cities to be at his beck and call if he needed them. She liked Cindy and Trish, and Amy wasn't annoyed this time that Bill could just take care of everything at the snap of a finger.

"That's perfect," Amy said, and Mabel cooed. Bill would have Cindy bring dresses for Mabel to try on as well, and if she wanted, Trish would do her hair, and Amy knew Mabel wanted.

"One more thing," Bill said. "Can I take the boys to the Yankees game tomorrow? We watched a lot of baseball together on the island, and they are really into it. Seems that Matt told them all about sports on the other island."

Amy remembered the picture she'd seen of William holding a crudely carved stick as though he was at bat, and she knew Bill was right. Matt was a regular guy in that way. He loved sports and he loved the Yankees. Amy cringed at the thought that Matt would miss taking them to their first Yankees game.

"I have the box, and you know DD and Jennie will help keep an eye on the boys." DD and Jennie were sisters in the box next to Bill's, and they hadn't missed a game in three years. They were lottery winners and salt of the earth.

Amy considered it for another minute, not sure why she was so worried about what Matt might want since he had ditched her and the boys.

"Boys," Amy called. "Want to go to a Yankees game with Uncle Bill tomorrow?"

CHAPTER 9

Matt loved clothes shopping since he had discovered weight lifting as a twenty-six year old. He had no money back then, but his tall, lithe frame fit perfectly in most attire and it made him feel confident. Matt was now in the tuxedo rental store to pick up a very expensive tuxedo, because although Sarah had invited him to a gala and told him to dress nice, he didn't yet have the money to purchase a tuxedo. He grimaced knowing he would be putting the rental on a second credit card.

The thought of money made him think of Bill Ruby again. Matt wanted to take the wire transfer of money Bill had offered to pay for the sunken airplane. But he couldn't, because if he did he would lose his pilot's license, and he'd gone through too many hours of training to chance it.

He still thought there might be a way out. His savings had dwindled in the last year because he hadn't had much work, and his credit card company was now calling and badgering him for payment. He was maxed out because the airplane company on Eleuthera Island charged him the max on his credit card as a first installment for the aircraft, and although he'd canceled the card, they were still investigating for fraud. His insurance company had called and he had denied that this was his claim, which was a lie. Matt didn't know what he was doing anymore, but he knew he would have fun at the gala tomorrow night with Sarah. She was a prize, and she was his.

Matt stood in front of the mirror and waited for the sales clerk to finish tying his bowtie. He'd never learned how to do that, but if he was going to marry Sarah and go to gala events, he thought he'd better learn soon. The sales clerk walked away, and Matt admired himself in the three-sided mirror. He noticed a man behind him watching and suddenly felt self-conscious. Matt turned around and stared back at the bleached blond and tanned man.

"Matt Cole," the man said with a friendly smile.

"Yes. Can I help you?" Matt smiled back, but there was something about this man that wasn't right. He was dressed down but in a very expensive jogging outfit, wearing five hundred dollar gym shoes, and he reeked L.A.

"Where would you like me to administer this DNA test?" the man asked, his eyes moving easily around the store. Matt's eyes followed, and he realized that they were alone in this area. Matt felt himself start to sweat.

"You have the wrong Matt Cole."

The man smiled and nodded. "No, you are the only Matt Cole I'm looking for. Recently flew to Ruby Island with three boys in the aircraft?"

Matt pulled at his collar, suddenly sweating. He wondered if his face was turning red. "I didn't crash. I landed the aircraft."

"Ah," the man said. "Well, we can do this back in your dressing room." He held out a small bag and Matt wondered what might be in a DNA kit, but he had no intention of finding out.

Matt turned back to look in the mirror. "I'm not taking a paternity test, so you can scamper back to Reynolds and let her know she's nuts." Matt could see the man nod in the mirror, and he smiled a half-smile and straightened his bowtie.

"Are you sure? It would be a lot simpler if you would just help me out here."

"Get lost, buddy."

The last word was barely out of Matt's mouth when the man darted forward. Matt saw a flash of blond hair and then the man's arm swung across his reflection in the mirror, and he thought the guy was taking a swing at him. He ducked to the side, but the guy grabbed Matt's hair and pulled.

"Ouch!" Matt yelled as he staggered away from the man. Blondie was smiling at Matt, a full inch of his hair pulled out at the root. Matt reached up and thought he could feel a bald spot on his head.

Blondie opened his bag and pulled a plastic baggie out, depositing the hair inside and zipping it closed.

"We can do this the easy way," he said.

"Get away from me!" Matt yelled. He figured the store clerk or other customers would come running back to see what was going on, but no one came. Matt stood up to his full height, ready to defend himself.

"Come on, mate," the guy said, feigning an Australian accent.

"I'm calling the police," Matt said, fumbling for his phone, but he was in the rental tux and his phone was in the changing room.

"No hard feelings," the guys said, and then he pulled a gun out.

At least Matt thought it was a gun. The metal glinted under the bright lights and he threw his hands up. "Don't shoot!" He squinted and froze in place.

"Don't be so dramatic," the guy said. He stepped forward and grabbed Matt's arm and then Matt saw that it was a staple gun. He tried to twist away, but Blondie was strong. He pressed Matt's left side hard into the wall and then jammed the staple gun against his right shoulder and pulled the trigger.

Matt felt a nail pierce through his skin and it felt like his shoulder was swelling up. "What the hell!" he screamed, and the guy stepped back and put his hands up.

"All done," Blondie said. "Calm down."

Matt's left hand went up to his right shoulder and he looked down. There was a small hole in the tuxedo jacket. "What did you do to me?" Matt asked.

"This little beauty was made for the military to give medical shots to their new recruits. It's kind of like a staple gun, but it delivers the shots." Blondie pulled a small needle from the front of the device and put it in a plastic baggie. "I use it to get a bit of blood for DNA testing."

"You ruined my jacket!" Matt complained.

"I asked nicely," Blondie said as he zipped up his bag and turned and left the shop.

AMY DRANK her third cup of coffee and realized she'd overdone it. She was already jumpy with all of the turmoil in her life.

"It's mine, it's mine!" Benji yelled as he chased Steven around the table and back out into the living room, both boys almost knocking her and her coffee over.

"Boys!" Amy yelled and cupped her forehead in her hands.

"Benji, Steven, come here," Mabel called with friendly authority in her voice.

"Yes, Aunt Mabel," Steven said, and Amy saw the boys walk into the darkroom. Amy sighed. She'd spent an hour in there this morning, but she still couldn't remember the moments that were in the photos. Amy moved to the door and watched as William told Mabel all about the island and his mom and dad.

Amy was so grateful to have the boys, and she didn't know where that emotion had come from, but she was truly happy to be their mother. She couldn't remember even kissing Matt though, and she was frustrated with her lack of memory. She leaned against the door of the dark room and watched Mabel with the boys.

Mabel pulled an old photo album off of the shelf and had the boys sit next to her on the twin bed that Amy had slept on.

"This is your mom when she was your age, and I swear you are the spitting image." Mabel tapped Steven's nose and turned the page, showing more photos of Amy as a child.

Amy's phone chimed and she saw a text from Bill. It was a photo of a vintage car he owned, and he said that he wanted to give it to William. He'd parked it in "Amy's garage" and it was ready whenever William wanted to take a spin. Amy grunted and bit her lip, and she texted back that she would be over in a bit if he was home. Bill said he would be home for the next two hours.

Amy took a deep breath to calm herself. She knew that Bill was trying to be nice, and this is just what he did. Bill Ruby marched in and took care of things. He spoiled everyone and it was charming, until it was overwhelming. Amy remembered how many gifts Bill had tried to give her when they dated and even in the time that they'd just been friends, and it was a bit too much.

He had once paid a food cart to sit outside her house for a week just in case Amy had wanted another taco, because she'd commented how much she'd liked their food. Another time, Bill had hired a personal assistant to travel to Chicago with her for a photo shoot, just to make sure Amy had everything she needed. She was pretty sure that the "assistant" had been a bodyguard because Amy was going to photograph a well-known rapper and "gansta" in the neighborhood he'd grown up in. It was endearing that Bill had wanted to take care of her, until it felt like she was being smothered.

"This is a photo of your mother at the Mount Everest base camp. Do you boys know what that is?" Mabel asked.

"Yes," William said, and Mabel gave an approving nod to Amy.

"They seem to be well-educated, Mabel, but Bill told them about Mount Everest," Amy admitted. The boys could read at least, and they were respectful. She wondered how she could have pulled that off while stranded on an island.

"That's Mom with Uncle Bill," Benji said, pointing to a picture in the back of the album.

Amy knew that they were seeing the magazine cutouts of her with Bill Ruby at celebrity events. Her mother had kept the file, and commented profusely that it was only so she could remember seeing her daughter dressed properly for once in her life. Amy didn't like to get decked out like Mabel did. It seemed like a chore, one that she'd done while in the jet-setter scene in her past. Amy groaned because she would be repeating the task tomorrow.

"Look how gorgeous she is, boys," Mabel commented. "They dated a couple of years ago," Mabel said and then cleared her throat. "Well now, I mean a couple of years before William was born."

Mabel smiled at the boys and Amy could tell that her mother's stomach was turning. Served her right, Amy thought. Mabel might have just gotten a glimpse of the turmoil Amy was feeling. How could one reconcile time when there seemed to be two different time lines at the same time? It was impossible, and Amy had been horrible at physics, so she would never figure it out. Before she could interject, Mabel simply closed the photo album.

"Who wants to hear what a record player sounds like?" Mabel asked.

"Me," the boys chimed in unison, although they most likely had no idea what that was. They followed Mabel upstairs.

"I'm jumping in the shower if there's any hot water left," Amy said as she went up behind them. Now that the boys had been introduced to indoor plumbing and discovered hot showers, it was impossible to get into either of the bathrooms.

When Amy was dressed, she heard the doorbell ring, so she went downstairs to answer, still in her bare feet.

"Amy!" her friend Lucy called, as her two young boys raced

past into the townhouse. Lucy stepped in and gave Amy an airy kiss on the cheek. "Boys, be on your best behavior," Lucy yelled.

"Come in," Amy said and closed the door. Lucy stepped into the front room and turned dramatically, her fashionable scarf floating in the breeze behind her.

"Amy, you little minx. You are going with Bill Ruby to the gala tomorrow night?"

Amy's mouth dropped open. It had been less than two hours since Bill had asked her to the gala, and although she knew Lucy was part of New York society, she couldn't believe how fast her friend had found that out.

There was a crash in the kitchen.

"Boys!" Lucy yelled. She flipped her silky brown hair and then tugged on Amy's arm, pulling her down on the sofa so Amy could tell her all about Bill Ruby.

"How could you know that?" Amy asked, less concerned with what the boys might be breaking in the kitchen.

"Well," Lucy said and leaned in, "Susan told Janice that she ran into Monica, and Monica said that Trish had to move her appointment up a couple of hours, and we all know that Trish only does that for one client."

"Okay," Amy said baffled at her friend's conclusion. "But how could you know that it meant me?"

"Oh, honey," Lucy said, pulling her mammoth-sized cell phone from her purse. "This was tweeted out yesterday. You were seen getting off of Bill's private jet with some kids."

Amy leaned in and looked at the picture. The photo wasn't great and it must have been taken with a very long lens, but sure enough, it was her and the boys walking from the plane to the car at the airport.

"Oh, God," Amy moaned, dropping her head to her hand. There was another crash and Lucy stood up.

"Boys," she called, disappearing down the hallway.

Amy groaned and flopped back on the couch, unable to believe how fast everything was moving.

～

"WHAT'S THIS?" Lucy yelled down the hall to Amy who was still flopped back on the couch.

"What broke?" Amy called back.

"What are these photos?"

Amy gasped and sat straight up. She would have told Lucy everything eventually, but she really didn't have the energy to get into it today.

"Mom! Aunt Mabel showed us how to use a record player," Benji called from upstairs. Amy could hear the rumble of footsteps trampling downstairs, and she stood up quickly to make her way down the hall toward Lucy before her boys could get there first. When she rounded the corner, Lucy had popped her head back out of the darkroom with her mouth wide open.

"Who was just yelling 'mom', because it wasn't my boys?"

As if on cue, Benji, William, and Steven appeared behind Amy.

"We heard big band jazz, Mom," Benji said as he wrapped his arms around Amy's waist.

Lucy pulled her wrist up to her face to look at her wristwatch. "I just saw you like a month ago, right?" she asked Amy, who tried to smile. Lucy looked at Benji and then stepped into the dark room and looked more closely at the photos. Most of the ones that were hanging up were the boys and Bill on Ruby Island. Amy had stacked the older ones on the desk because they both confused her and infuriated her. She didn't need to see photos of her and Matt creating a romance that neither of them could remember.

A chair knocked over in the kitchen and Lucy's boys began to fight.

"William, can you keep an eye on them?" Amy asked. Lucy's

boys always found a way to break something when they popped over, and today they were doing their best to set a record.

"I know, I know," William huffed as though he'd been asked to do this a thousand times already.

"Oh my God," Lucy said, and Amy moved into the dark room behind her. "Bill Ruby had your test tube babies and they look just like you." Lucy pointed at a picture of William. "This one's too old, though. He's definitely before your 'friendship'," Lucy did air quotes with her hands, "with Bill Ruby."

Amy heard Mabel laugh from the hallway. "I thought the same thing, dear," she said to Lucy.

Amy said defensively, "Bill did not clone me." In fact, Bill had been nothing but kind to her and the boys, and she was getting tired of everyone picking on him.

"Ooh, I didn't think of that," Lucy said. "Wasn't he obsessed with you?" Lucy asked.

"Head over heels," Mabel called from the kitchen.

"Enough, Mabel," Amy said, and she closed the door to the dark room.

"Lucy, I have to tell you something, and you are going to think I'm insane, but just hear me out."

"We both know you are," Lucy said with a wink. Amy was glad to have her oldest friend in on the secret because she needed someone to talk to.

Amy grabbed the folder that held the pictures of her and Matt and opened it on the counter next to Lucy. They both looked at a photo of Amy and Matt sitting on the sand, Amy in her bikini leaning back into Matt as he smiled at her. The photo held all of Amy's fantasies about her and Matt when she'd had a crush on him back before the island.

"Sexy mama!" Lucy said and nudged her friend with her elbow. Then she leaned in closer and asked, "Hey, isn't that the guy dating the news anchor? What's her name?" Lucy pondered this while Amy wondered how her friend could place people so quickly. Really, it was a gift.

"That's Matt Cole," Amy said.

"That's Matt Cole!" Lucy repeated, and then she made a cat purring sound. "When you told me about him, I can't believe I didn't cyber-stalk him. I must be losing my touch. He's delicious, Amy. What is this photo shoot? You don't ever pose in front of the camera."

Amy didn't answer, but she slid through the photos of them before she was pregnant, during, with baby William, and then baby Steven, and Lucy's comments ended as soon as she'd seen the first photo of her friend's bulging belly.

"Amy, what is this?" she whispered.

Amy let Lucy shuffle through the photos as she explained everything as well as she could. Lucy knew about Amy's crush on Matt, although she knew it as a small casual crush and not the looming aching secret love she now realized it had been.

Amy talked about the flash of light, the boys materializing in the back of the airplane, and through her time with Bill Ruby.

"Oh my God. It's unbelievable," Lucy said. They were silent for a few minutes while Lucy strolled around the dark room and looked at more photos of Bill and the boys that were still hung up.

"It looks like the boys have really taken to Bill," Lucy said. "You know, there are a lot of photos of the first boy, but barely any of the other two. But, that's how it is with children. The first is doted on, and then life happens."

"Well, I was stranded on an island and there really wasn't anywhere to pick up more film," Amy said defensively, while she made a mental note to take a lot of photos of Steven and Benji.

"So, where is this Matt Cole? I want to meet him."

Amy stood and put the folder back on the desk. "Well, as you said, he's engaged to Sarah Robinson, and so this is all a bit much for him."

"That's right, Sarah Robinson. I've seen them at some parties. They are a very good-looking couple."

"Lucy, you're not helping."

"I'm sorry, Ames," Lucy said. She hugged Amy. "Listen, you are going to a gala with Bill Ruby. You look like you had some fun on the island with him, and the boys get along with him. So if you were looking for my advice, I'd say go in that direction. Heck, if you were with Bill you wouldn't even have to think about child support from this Matt Cole."

Amy's hand went up to her face as there was another crash outside the door. "William!" she called.

"Boys!" Lucy yelled at the same time as she grabbed her purse and left the room.

Amy didn't bother to look at what was happening. She was in a haze and hadn't even thought about having to ask Matt for child support.

"I'll call you after the gala!" Lucy said, and Amy could hear the boy's trampling feet heading for the front door.

Amy looked at the photos of her boys and Bill again. He was a good man and she really liked him a lot, but the thought of Bill made her remember the car. She took a deep breath and headed down the hall. "Mabel, boys, I'm going to run an errand!"

Matt stepped out of the car and looked up at the brownstone. He'd been here only once before to pick up film for an article that was at deadline when Reynolds was sick. He hesitated on the sidewalk this time remembering the three boys' faces as they looked at him from the backseat of the airplane. He hadn't thought about seeing them again. He'd been so angry at the aggressive, surprise DNA test that he'd come here in a fit of anger.

He pulled out his phone to call another Uber and turned to leave, but then he reconsidered. He could face the boys if just to let Reynolds know that she couldn't assault him with a DNA test. It was outrageous!

"No, no, no," Matt said to himself and turned back to the building, almost bowling Reynolds over as she came down the stairs.

"Great," she said, and she walked right past him.

Matt grunted and jogged to catch up. "Reynolds, wait up."

"Oh, now you want to talk to me?" she asked sarcastically under her breath, but loud enough for Matt to hear. "Did you finally come here to see the boys? William and Steven are holding it together, but Benji not so much." She glanced back at him and he didn't respond, so she moved on.

Matt walked behind Amy for a full block because he didn't really know what to say to her. When she got to the corner, she looked back and saw him, and in a huff she turned the corner and walked another block.

"Will you be following me around all day today, Matt? Or did you have something to say?"

"I have a lot of something to say to you," he said. His blood boiled when he thought of Blondie stabbing him with a staple gun, but he got distracted when Amy stepped up to the brown garage door that was built into the front of a new townhome. Private garages were impossible to find in New York City, and Matt was stunned. Reynolds punched some numbers into the keypad, and the door started to open.

"What is this place?" he asked.

"This is my garage," she said.

"You keep a car?" he asked, and she thought he sounded impressed.

"I know, it's not practical in New York City. I keep a space in a garage, and there is a car in it," she answered. Amy didn't know how to tell Matt that Bill had rented a space in this two-car garage on a ten year contract when they'd been dating, and he'd apparently not dissolved the contract, because he'd said the code was still set as her birthday. Amy didn't want to think about the millions of dollars this garage must have cost Bill over a ten year period.

She shook her head when she saw the small green car with a blue racing stripe down the middle.

"Wow, nice car," Matt said, and Amy nodded. She had always loved this car, but it wasn't practical to drive in the city, and she was afraid that it would get scratched.

"It's William's car, or at least it was for a minute."

"William doesn't even drive!" Matt complained. Then he reconsidered because he really didn't know the boy at all, but he seemed too young to have a license. "Does he?"

"A little. Bill showed him how on the island."

"Wait a minute," Matt said moving around the car. "Is this the…"

Amy cut him off. "Yes, this is the 1978 Mini Cooper from *Last Road to Nowhere*, and no, I won't let William accept this gift, so you don't have to worry."

"I'm not worried," Matt said. It struck him how easy Reynolds talked about the boy. It was like he was really hers, and she'd been parenting him all these years.

"He's going to be mad at you," Matt commented.

"He'll get over it," Amy said, stopping and giving Matt a warning stare. "And I'm sure Bill will let William drive it any time he wants."

Matt put his hands up in surrender. "I was talking about the boy."

"Really? You were talking about one of the boys that you ditched and haven't called or come to visit even once?" she said sarcastically.

"You know, Reynolds? I used to think you were nothing like regular women, but I was wrong."

"Gee, thanks," she said opening a lockbox on the wall with another code and pulling the keys out of the box.

"You just grabbed onto this like it's some kind of fairy tale with these kids, and I don't know what you're trying to push me into."

"Push you into!" Amy yelled. "I don't know what happened on that plane, Matt, but I'm not a witch or a sorcerer who can just conjure up three boys. You were with me, for God's sake. You tell me what happened."

"You had some guy jump me with a DNA test, that's what

happened! He stabbed me in the arm with a needle and ruined my tuxedo jacket."

She stared at him for a minute and bit her lip because she had no idea what he was talking about. "Well you look just fine to me." Amy moved around the car toward the driver's side, but Matt blocked her.

"You've got to let this go, Amy. I mean we're both losing our minds, right?" Amy glanced at his dimpled chin and looked up into Matt's eyes. His arms were outstretched in question, but it looked like he might hug her, and for a moment, Amy imagined herself in his arms pressed up to his chest. She hated Matt right now with his beautiful sideways smile and his ignoring their children.

Amy mumbled. "I don't even know what to say to you right now." She tried to sidestep him to get in the car, but Matt snatched the keys from her hands.

"I'll drive," Amy said through clenched teeth while trying to squash the animalistic rage welling up inside.

"I can drive. You don't want to scratch this baby," Matt told her as he swung his tall body lithely into the driver's seat.

"You're going to start picking on my driving now?"

"I've got this, just relax."

"I hate it when people tell me to relax," Amy said. "Get out of the car, Matt, I've got things to do today."

Matt had inserted the key and he tried to turn the ignition, but nothing happened. "Dammit!" Matt said as he pounded the steering wheel.

"Take it easy, I need to return this in one piece," Amy complained.

Matt stood up and walked around the front of the car, seating himself in the passenger seat.

Amy looked at Matt wryly. "Really? You fly airplanes, but you can't drive stick?"

Amy slid into the driver's seat and buckled up before

engaging the clutch and starting the car. She eased out of the garage and pressed the garage remote that was clipped to the floor mat.

When Amy pulled onto the side street, she turned to Matt. "Just go, Matt. Be free. Live your life and be happy, if you can."

"Don't bring Sarah into this," he barked.

"Ooh, touchy much?" Amy asked. "I didn't bring your fiancé into this conversation, I just told you to be happy. Of course, maybe you're just the type of person who can't be happy." Amy drove, purposefully popping the clutch in second gear, which caused the car to lurch forward.

"Ha!" He said, and then a few moments passed in silence. "Maybe the problem with you is that you are more happy than anyone else. Maybe your level of happiness is abnormal, not my level of unhappiness. You know, sometimes I'm just living here." He stopped short, realizing that he was yelling. The irony wasn't lost on Matt that he was grumbling about being happy, because if he would admit it, on some level he wasn't happy at all.

Amy drove a few blocks in silence. She turned the corner and headed down Park Avenue toward Bill's New York penthouse. She pulled up to the valet who opened her door, and the doorman opened the passenger door.

"Are you in or are you out?" Amy asked. She meant the visit with Bill, but once the words were out of her mouth, she knew she'd meant more.

Matt stepped out of the car and looked at the building.

"It's Bill's place," she said before he had time to ask.

"Of course it is," Matt answered somberly. Bill Ruby was the last person he wanted to see right now.

"I'm out," he said, and Amy felt the sting.

"This is Bill Ruby's car," Amy said to the valet.

"Of course, miss," the valet said, and Amy felt a pang of jealousy realizing how easy he'd accepted that a woman would be out driving one of Bill's cars alone.

Amy shrugged it off as she stepped toward the curb. She spent a lot of time in Manhattan, and yet she looked up at the imposing twenty-five-story building. It was a restored brick building that had giant windows on each level, and it held all of the charm of the original design but with a flare of wealth in the new shiny features.

Amy looked to her right in time to see Matt walk away without a backward glance. He turned the corner out of sight. "Typical," she said to herself.

She walked through the revolving door and crossed to the elevator. She shook her head when she recognized Bill's butler, Donnelly, standing in the lobby of the high rise. He was in his full black butler attire and he looked out of place in the lobby.

"I can ride the elevator alone," she said.

"It's so nice to see you too, Miss Reynolds. No boys in tow today?"

Amy shook her head as they entered the elevator.

"Mr. Rogers' floor, please," the butler said to the elevator attendant who swiped a card over a flat black pad and pressed two buttons on the keypad.

"Mr. Rogers?" Amy asked, knowing Bill liked to use race car driver's names in place of his own for privacy.

"The staff and I have been having some fun with him since you showed up with the children."

"Yes, but you've been having no fun. Am I right?" Donnelly had been nothing but courteous to Amy and the boys, but she knew he liked being employed by a jet-setter.

He avoided answering the question so Amy asked another. "I've only seen you at the homes in the Caribbean and Los Angeles. What brings you here?"

Donnelly cleared his throat. "I'm here in case you need help with the boys," he said sincerely.

"You?" She sang and then cleared her throat, and the elevator attendant gave a quiet hoot. "Sorry, I assumed you didn't like children."

"Mr. Rogers pointed out that I am a familiar face to them. He thought it might make them comfortable in their adjusting to society."

"That's very thoughtful," Amy said.

Donnelly smiled as the elevator doors opened. "Mr. Rogers is a thoughtful person."

Amy stepped from the elevator and the beautiful yet sparse decor took her breath away.

"Amy, it's great to see you. I didn't think I'd get the pleasure until tomorrow when I pick up the boys for the Yankees game."

"You've redecorated," Amy said, admiring the space. It looked like it came out of a magazine.

"Last year," Bill answered, and Amy wondered if a woman had convinced him to make the change from his bachelor pad tones to this minimalist chic. It was none of her business, and she didn't trust headlines for facts, but she knew Bill had dated several models and actresses since they had been an item, and she wished they hadn't grown apart.

"I like it," Amy said, running her hand over the back of the couch.

"I'm glad," Bill said with a heart-pounding gorgeous smile. He came around the couch and met her, kissing her tenderly on both cheeks. He was rubbing Amy's arms, and she loved the warmth of his touch. She drew in his smell, the perfect mix of his sweet sweat and cologne. They looked eye to eye, Bill brushing away her tousled bangs.

"I brought the car back," she said in a calmer tone than she'd intended. They were standing close together, and it was comfortable.

"It's not yours to give back," he said, his perfect lips parting in a smile that exposed his perfect, white teeth.

Amy swatted him in the chest and was reminded of his hard muscles when her hand hit his shirt.

"He's too young to own a car, Bill, especially a classic. It's fun to drive, though," Amy admitted. All of the anger toward Bill for taking over the situation again had flowed out of her, but she did have to make sure he understood his place.

"He'll get his license soon enough," Bill said.

In four years, she thought, but she didn't want to argue.

Amy pulled back and strolled around the couch, sitting down and looking at the building across the street. Anyone might expect Bill Ruby to take the penthouse suite, but he didn't like being on the top floors. He wasn't afraid of heights at all, but he didn't like to get stuck on long elevator rides as people got on and off of the elevator. He liked the middle floor of this building because it was far enough away from the street as to not get all of the traffic noise, yet low enough to be a short and direct ride up. Amy knew he used the stairs for the exercise when he was alone.

Bill sat next to Amy. "What can I do for you?" he asked sincerely.

"Bill, you have been nothing but gracious during this whole mess. Can you just spend some time with me and the boys and don't overdo it?"

"It's the popcorn machine all over again, isn't it?" he asked.

Amy laughed. "Something like that," she said.

When they had first dated and they watched movies in his private home theater, Amy had commented that she missed going to the movie theater because there was nothing like movie theater popcorn. The next time she'd visited his home outside of L.A., there was a full candy counter with popcorn maker installed along with an attendant to take their order. It had been flattering at the time, but also excessive. Amy had asked Bill why he didn't just send someone to pick up a bucket of popcorn at the local theater, and he'd laughed and said it wouldn't be the same, but she could tell by the slight crinkle in his eyebrow that he'd never thought of going the simple route.

"Do you still have it?" Amy asked.

"I had to remove it. That butter is a killer on the waistline." He patted his stomach and Amy frowned, worried about her own waistline and the elegant dresses she would be trying on in a few hours.

CHAPTER 11

Cindy and Trish had worked their magic, and Amy's boys were amazed at their mom's transformation. They could hardly believe that she was the same person in such a beautiful gown, and she was wearing makeup, which they'd never seen her wear before. Bill promised that he'd get her home early and he high-fived each of them on the way out the door.

Amy could see that their time was well spent at the baseball game that afternoon, and she was glad they were all getting along. Maybe Bill could be the right father figure if Matt was never going to bother showing up.

Mabel was also gorgeous in her elegant evergreen gown and small cap fixed with the throwback bit of veil over one eye. The boys danced around her chanting "Auntie Mabel", and although she was gorgeous, Amy hoped that her mother couldn't actually pass as her sister.

Bill's limo was waiting outside, and Amy tried to delicately climb in. She felt like a princess when she wore a gown, but she also worried she'd accidentally tear the material. Bill slid in next to her and the driver closed the door and quickly pulled away into traffic.

121

"Thanks again for taking the boys to the game. They had so much fun."

Bill was bright-eyed, but Amy knew that if she'd gone to the baseball game, she would be exhausted from the outing. Bill was always full of energy and full of life, and he'd probably gone home, lifted weights, and drank a power smoothie before picking her up.

"It was my pleasure, Amy. You did a great job raising them. They behaved perfectly, and we had a blast."

Amy's face twisted up for a moment. She couldn't remember even one minute of raising the boys, and she still didn't know how to reconcile that.

"Yes, I did a great job raising them," she said disappointed, and Bill squeezed her hand. She hoped he couldn't tell that she was thinking of Matt at that moment.

In less than ten minutes, they turned the corner to the hotel and Amy's eyes opened wide when she suddenly remembered Matt's visit.

"What is it?" Bill asked.

"Matt came by yesterday. He was extremely angry. Something about a DNA test?"

Bill nodded and smiled. "Gary's in town."

"Mmm-hmmm," Amy said with a smile. She liked Gary even though he seemed like a hanger-on, and although she didn't want Matt hurt, she was glad she would have the evidence she needed to convince him that the boys were his, too. She wasn't pushing for a relationship with him, but she had no intention of letting Matt off the hook with the boys. It broke her heart when the boys asked where dad was, and they deserved to have their father in their life.

It was all so confusing, and Amy knew she wouldn't have made it this far without Bill. She would have lost her mind, and she knew it.

When the limousine pulled up to the hotel and Amy saw all of the photographers and the red carpet, she took a deep breath.

"It's been a while," Bill said, taking Amy's hand. "Are you ready?"

Amy nodded and the car stopped. A valet waited outside with his hand on the doorknob and then Bill knocked twice on the window and the door whipped open. A thousand flashbulbs went off, and Bill lithely swept out of the car. Amy could hear the energy of the crowd calling his name, but he ignored them, turning back to Amy to help her out of the limousine.

She slid from the seat and Bill pulled her up, and Amy was once again standing on the red carpet next to him.

"Who's the girl?" someone called from the crowd of paparazzi, but Bill ignored it.

Amy looped her arm in his, and they made their way up the red carpet. She was in Bill's bubble now, and even out here among the flashbulbs and swarm of action, he was solid and steady and calm, waving here and there to reporters he knew, and somehow still making Amy feel protected. Protected, of course, until twenty minutes into the cocktail hour when Matt arrived with his fiancé.

MATT WAS glad to be at the gala this evening. His fiancé was stunning, and much of New York society was attending. Matt smiled and nodded at people Sarah was talking to, and he enjoyed his bourbon. Everyone was gracious and having a good time, and Matt liked feeling part of the festivities.

"Hi, Dad," Sarah said, kissing Charley on the cheek.

"Mr. Robinson," Matt said as he shook Charley's hand. Matt tried to smile and look Charley in the eye, but he still owed the magazine an article he hadn't even started writing, and he was terrified that Charley would find out what happened on Ruby

Island. He was also petrified that Charley and Sarah would find out about the boys.

The boys, Matt thought. *Where the hell had they come from?* He smiled at Charley and drank his bourbon down and tried for the thousandth time to forget about the flash of white light and the scared voices of the boys who had appeared out of thin air. Matt felt an eerie chill just thinking about it, and he shook off the goosebumps.

"Matt," Charley said with a tight handshake. "Shouldn't you be working tonight?"

"A-ha, very funny Mr. Robinson," Matt said with a bright smile, trying to lighten up the comment. Charley stared at Matt for a second too long, letting Matt know that he wanted his article, and then he too smiled for the sake of his daughter.

"Daddy, Matt's escorting me tonight. He can work tomorrow."

"I know, darling," Charley said. He kissed Sarah on the cheek and then he patted Matt on the upper arm and moved away. Matt grimaced at the light pat on his arm because it was right in the place where the crazy man in the tuxedo shop had stabbed him with the staple gun-like blood extractor. Matt rubbed his arm and clenched his teeth and vowed if he ever saw that guy again, he would punch him in the face. He also vowed that he would let Reynolds have it the next time he saw her.

Sarah squeezed Matt's arm tightly and squealed, "Oh my God, it's Bill Ruby! You know him, Matt. You have to introduce us." She was bouncing slightly in her heels like a child who just spotted a clown with a bundle of balloons, and Matt looked over to see Bill Ruby and his date moving through the crowd. He grit his teeth and sighed and wondered why he couldn't get away from this guy.

"Come on, Matt," Sarah said, pulling on his arm. "Introduce us. I'm going to ask him for an interview."

Matt dutifully followed Sarah as they wound through the crowd to Bill Ruby. Matt noticed that Bill had a knockout on his arm in an elegant yellow dress. The girl was looking away and Matt couldn't see her face, but he assumed she was a model and was probably gorgeous. Bill had chosen wisely because his date was only about an inch taller than him, but Matt didn't pay much attention because all eyes were on Bill.

"Matt, good to see you again," Bill said graciously.

Matt nodded and tried to smile, but he couldn't. Matt had rented a fine tuxedo, but megastar Bill Ruby had on an elegant, black tuxedo that had a shiny material on the front of the lapels. It was utterly original, and it made Matt fume.

"Bill," Matt said, "I would like you to meet my fiancé, Sarah Robinson."

Sarah chirped when Bill took her hand gently and shook it for about ten seconds too long. Matt sighed and stared at Bill's tuxedo, trying to place the fabric.

"Sarah, it's a great pleasure to meet you," Bill said, his dashing smile melting everyone within a twenty foot radius. "When I met Matt, he couldn't stop talking about you."

Matt's face turned red because he couldn't remember if he had mentioned Sarah to Bill when he was on the island. Sarah patted Matt on the chest and nodded, but she was speechless for the first time ever.

"Sarah wants to interview you," Matt said.

"I do," Sarah croaked.

"That would be great," Bill said as he leaned in toward Sarah. "A tell-all, as it were. I'm sure Matt can give you some notes." The two laughed and Matt turned from red to pale. He hadn't interviewed Bill, and he had no intention of doing that now. He needed to find out about the airplane though, and he hoped he could get Bill alone for a minute this evening.

"It was wonderful to meet you," Bill said as his date pulled on his hand to steer him away from the couple.

"It was my pleasure," Sarah gushed. Then she added dryly, "I didn't expect to see you here, Amy."

"Yes, well..." Amy managed, turning her face forward and looking at Sarah and Matt for the first time.

~

AS SARAH TURNED to walk away, Matt's mouth fell open and he did a double take, looking at her face for the first time. He was stunned the woman in yellow was Reynolds. She was beautiful, and she was with Bill Ruby. Her hair was blonde but with brown highlights now and pulled back tightly. He didn't know you could get short hair to pull back, but hers was in a fake bun with some brown strands elegantly framing her face.

"Reynolds?" Matt gasped as Sarah pulled on his hand.

"She's getting away," Bill said with a wink and a smile, and Matt turned to stumble after his fiancé. As he went, he wondered if Bill might have been referring to Reynolds.

~

AMY GUSHED when Liam Neeson hugged her, and she all but forgot about Matt. He hadn't even looked at her when Bill and Sarah were talking, and although she had tried her best to look away and pretend she was surveying the room around her, it had really angered her when she realized that he hadn't even recognized her.

They all took their seats and, before dinner, they talked about raising children, and Amy had stuttered when Liam remembered she hadn't had any children last time they'd met. Bill was quick to think, and he said that she'd adopted to save her from having to tell the unrealistic story.

They joked with Bill about turning into a family man, and he was sincere about his affection for the boys, which made Amy glad. She felt like she'd been hit in the stomach though, when she noticed Matt looking their way.

∼

DINNER WAS ENJOYABLE FOR MATT, although he kept looking over at Bill Ruby, who had his arm around Reynolds all night. Matt wondered if he would have eventually recognized her on his own. He put his arm around Sarah and smiled, squeezing her shoulder, but he kept returning his gaze to the other table. Reynolds was laughing with Liam Neeson like they were old friends, and Matt was thoroughly jealous. He wanted to be best buddies with celebrities and go through life without a care. And where were the boys tonight? Had she left them with a stranger? He told himself he didn't really care about that, but his temper was rising, and he stood and moved to the nearest open bar when dessert was served.

"Matt Cole," he heard from behind, and he swung around with a smile on his face until he saw who was addressing him. It was Bill Ruby walking toward him. The superstar had a smug expression, and Matt looked around for Reynolds, but he didn't see her anywhere.

"Bill Ruby," Matt replied, trying to be courteous. It hurt to fake smile after a minute, so Matt stopped trying so hard.

"I owe you, Matt," Ruby said, looking around the room.

"You're welcome," Matt said. He was annoyed, wondering what Ruby was talking about.

"Here you are," Bill said, taking a small card out of his jacket pocket and handing it to Matt.

Matt looked at the card and it took him a second to realize that it was his credit card. The last time Matt had seen it was when he'd rented the small airplane on Eleuthera Island. Matt turned the card around in his hand and looked at Bill.

"Now we are square. The charges have been reversed and you'll see a credit on your statement. I took care of the airplane, and no one knows it was you, so you don't have to worry about your pilot's license. Your flight plan and insurance card and all of the documents have been destroyed, and we're done here."

"Then, thank you," Matt said. He was hesitant. Bill Ruby had just done an enormous kindness by paying for the aircraft, and Matt was in the clear. He should have been relieved, but he wondered why instead he felt like he had just stuck his head into a lion's mouth.

"Please, Matt. It was my pleasure. I owed you one for landing Amy and those boys safely on my island. It's the least I could do."

Reynolds appeared from the lobby and Matt almost waved to her, but she spotted Ruby and he smiled wide and nodded at her.

"Where's your fiancé gone off to?" Bill asked. Matt looked at the movie star in his perfect tuxedo made out of some fabric he'd never seen. His hair was perfect, his teeth were perfect, and his skin was perfect. There was no way Matt could ever write that article because he hated Bill Ruby.

Reynolds was weaving her way through the crowd toward them, and Ruby patted Matt on the right shoulder in the exact spot that was sore, and Matt grit his teeth.

"So, your business with Amy is concluded," he said with a wide grin. "Have a good year."

~

"A moment, please," Amy growled as she met the two men in her life. She was looking at Matt, and he was actually grateful when Bill replied.

"You can have more than a moment, Amy." He put his hand on the small of her back to escort her away, but he could see that she wasn't going to let it go, so Bill cleared his throat. "I'll go bid Liam and the others adieu."

Bill turned and walked away, and Amy stared at Matt, her eyes boring into his.

"Adieu?" Matt asked sarcastically. "Who says that?"

"A gentleman says that," Amy raged, and she took a champagne glass from a passing tray.

"I'm a gentleman," Matt said. He lightly tugged at the ends of his bowtie, careful not to undo the knot because Sarah had to tie it for him. He gawked at Amy for a moment and then a soft smile crossed his face. She was beautiful. A knockout really, in this gorgeous yellow dress with her curly hair pulled up like that.

"You, a gentleman?" Amy retorted. "A gentleman wouldn't have badgered a girl into taking an unsafe flight. A gentleman would have finished the trip via boat with her. And he sure as heck wouldn't have left her on that island alone with those three boys. With our three boys!" she corrected herself.

Matt looked around uncomfortably and his head jerked quick, like a bird. Sarah always took a long time in the ladies room, but he knew she would be back any second. And Charley was here, too. He knew that he was starting to crumble, and he hoped he didn't look crazy.

"You were hardly alone," he said, and he pulled at his collar. The room was suddenly hot.

"He was being gracious," Amy said of Bill Ruby.

"Gracious?" Matt disagreed. "He was neurotic with his staff buzzing about him and his shirt opened to show his perfectly tanned six pack abs."

"A great body is neurotic?" Amy asked.

"He was all aloof and cool. I mean, we had just told him that we didn't even know where those boys came from, and he acted like it was perfectly normal!"

"Well, you may be prone to lying, but Bill trusts me," she retorted.

"Sarah was too good for me. That's what he said on the island, right?" Matt laughed out loud, but Amy was too angry to be hurt.

"Listen, Matt. I don't think I originally came over here to argue with you."

"Then why are you?"

"I guess you just bring out the best in me," Amy said sarcastically. "When are you going to come over to see the boys?"

Matt looked at her dumbfounded, and Amy almost cried. He really didn't care at all about any of them.

"Don't you have good old Bill to take care of you?"

Amy bit her lip and allowed the anger to run over her because she was worried she might start crying right then and there. "That's right, because Bill is a gentleman and already a better father than you."

Matt gulped down his bourbon. He'd wanted an interview with Bill Ruby for a long time. He'd tried to get onto Ruby Island for three years, and he hated the three hours that he'd spent there.

"For your information, he's been nothing but decent to William, Steven and Benji." Amy's chin quivered, and she thought that she might cry. It bothered her. They stared at each other in silence for a long moment until Amy turned her chin up and walked away. Matt turned in the other direction and walked straight to the nearest bar.

CHAPTER 12

*A*my woke on the small twin bed that was in the corner of her dark room. The red light glowed dimly in the room, and it had allowed her to sleep soundly until she'd had a dream about Matt. She'd been enjoying herself until she heard the voices of children, and that had woken her up.

She listened for the sounds of the house, but no one was calling her, and Amy realized that the voices had been in her dream. She sat up, and when she saw the yellow dress hung over the back of the desk chair, she covered her eyes with her fingertips.

It should have been a wonderful evening, and there were parts that were really nice, but Amy was drowning in an overall sadness. She didn't want to be attracted to Matt, but seeing him in his tuxedo made her hold her breath, and she felt a bit of shame because he was engaged. On top of which, she knew that the improbable was true and she somehow had three sons with Matt.

There had been no romance that either of them could remember, but she'd seen the photos and heard the stories from the boys, and there was a world inside the Bermuda Triangle where they had been in love with each other. Her feelings for Matt had morphed in less than a month from silent crush to outright anger at him for ignoring her and the boys. It was exhausting.

Amy heard the boys laughing and she wondered what they were up to. She pulled on her sweatpants and left the darkroom, switching on the overhead lights and ignoring the photos hung on the strings all around her.

"Who was that on Bill Ruby's arm last night? She doesn't look happy. Doesn't she realize she's with Bill Ruby?" Amy heard a voice on the television mocking her. She rounded the corner to the family room and saw a photo on TV of her and Bill after they'd gotten out of the limousine. As much as Amy didn't love getting decked out like Mabel did, she thought that she looked good.

Amy looked at her mom and the faces of her three boys and she tried to smile, but she felt as though she'd been caught with another man, and she was horrified.

"Mabel, turn that off!" Amy said when she saw the old photos of her and Bill begin to scroll on the screen.

The morning talk show host gushed over the photos. "We tracked her down, and it looks like she's his old flame, Amy Reynolds."

"What's an old flame, Auntie Mabel?" Benji asked.

"Auntie Mabel, still?" Amy asked as she turned the TV off.

"Yes, like the movie *Auntie Mame* with Rosalind Russell. I always loved that movie."

Amy noticed that Mabel had two tablets open to photos of her and Bill, and her face turned red.

"Old flame is like an old friend," Amy told Benji.

"I doubt that," William answered.

Amy closed the tablets. "Those tabloids are vultures, you shouldn't be looking at this!"

William said, "That's what Auntie Mabel said, too, but it was already on when I turned on the TV."

"And the tablets?" Amy asked Mabel with a direct stare. Mabel shrugged and hugged Benji, giving him a kiss on the head.

Amy wanted to scream at her mother, but she sat down and took a deep breath. "I don't want to upset you boys."

"We're not upset," Steven said. He was writing in a notebook with a pencil, and he was always doing that now. Amy could see that his letters and words had grown tenfold since they'd met.

"Mabel said that you went out to this place so that you could talk to Dad," William said hopefully.

"I did see your father last night," Amy said.

"Is Daddy coming over today?" Benji asked as he played with Mabel's earring.

"Your Dad is busy right now," she said, trying to keep the tremor from her voice. She was heartbroken for these kids. It was the same worn-out excuse Amy had been giving the boys for three weeks since Matt had left them on Ruby Island. Amy moved in front of the couch and sat on the antique coffee table, but Mabel didn't comment.

Benji said, "Mom, I miss the island. Dad was there and we had a lot of fun. Like that time we did the long jump contest on the beach and Dad threw me to the end and I won!"

Amy tried to remember, but she shook her head in defeat.

"William, Steven, Benji," Amy said in all seriousness, "you know how I couldn't remember anything about our lives together? Well, your dad can't remember either. Those pictures of Uncle Bill and myself, they are from my past before your father and I fell in love and made a family." Amy looked at their faces hardly able to comprehend what she was even saying, because in truth it would have all been happening at the same time.

"I know it's really difficult for you, but he's just going to need some time to come around."

William and Steven stared at Amy but didn't say a word. It was Benji who broke her heart. He started to cry and threw himself at Amy. She caught him in her arms and moved over to the couch.

"Daddy always tells me a story before bed, and now I'm never going to see him again!" Benji cried. Amy hugged him tightly, but she didn't know what to say.

Steven started to cry too, but he silently wiped his tears away and ran upstairs. Amy looked to William, but he shrugged and turned the TV back on, changing the channel. Amy watched him for a minute. He had a serious and faraway look on his face. It was Matt's look, and she too had to fight back tears.

Mabel moved to the kitchen and when Benji had been consoled enough to settle down and become interested in the planetary documentary that William was watching, Amy went to talk to her mom.

"Poor kids," Mabel said offering Amy a cup of coffee. Amy took the cup and then pushed it away to put her head down on the table and cry. She hated herself for the tears and instantly wiped them away.

"I don't know what's wrong with me," Amy said wiping her face on a napkin.

"You're tough, Amy, but give yourself a break," Mabel told her. Amy couldn't remember the last time she had cried in front of her mom. Mabel never approved of it when Amy was young, so she had toughened up. She was surprised at the concession Mabel had given her today, but Amy had noticed a change in her mom since the boys had arrived.

Amy tried to grin and sipped her coffee.

"Why don't you fight for him? Go find their dad and stake your claim."

"He's engaged."

"I don't care," Mabel said patting her hand on the table. "It's not the right thing to say, but really, Amy, I don't care that he's engaged. Fight for him. You have three children together."

"We can't remember, Mabel. We can't remember falling in love and having three sons. Thirteen years that never existed don't make us a couple. I mean, if people who remember falling in love separate, how are we supposed to have a relationship when we don't even have the memories?"

"Arranged marriages last a lifetime. How do you explain that?"

Amy smiled. "How do you think of these things, Mom?"

Mabel sighed at the 'mom' reference but let it go.

"I know you were hurt when your engagement ended. The scoundrel cheated on you and you were devastated, but this is different. Matt's fiancé is engaged to a man who by the grace of God has three wonderful sons, and she has no idea. Is that fair to her to be lied to?"

"I don't know," Amy said, and it was the most honest answer she'd given in weeks. She didn't seem to know anything anymore.

LAST NIGHT MATT loved having Sarah on his arm, but today it just didn't seem like it was enough. Her voice grated on him this morning. He'd woken up in her spacious hi-rise apartment in midtown with floor to ceiling windows. He usually found this place exciting with the beautiful white light playing off the white furniture and the shined hard wood floors. Today he was hung over though, and even with the pillow on his head, Matt could hear the click, click, click of Sarah's shoes.

He knew it was after eight because each morning Sarah exercised for an hour, then showered and primped for another hour, and she always had her skirt-bottomed business suit with high heels on by eight. Matt didn't know why she wore her shoes in her apartment, and he'd always loved the way she looked, but this morning the click, click amplified his headache, and he growled into the pillow before rising.

Matt cursed himself for getting drunk. He never drank that much anymore. He'd started the evening drunk at the fundraiser because of Reynolds, and the night had gone downhill from there. When they had returned to Sarah's apartment and he couldn't be intimate with her, Sarah had snapped at him and it was annoying. Not being able to perform was terrifying for Matt, and he had written it off to the alcohol. But truth be told, if he would admit it to himself, it opened up criticism for all of the things that Sarah did that had gotten under his skin. They'd been going along so good until Matt went to that darn, cursed Ruby island.

Matt pulled the pillow off his face and let his eyes adjust to the white light. He loved Sarah. He wouldn't have proposed to her if he didn't, but lately it grated on him when she snapped at him. She had always been the same since he met her, and he had tried to ignore his changing feelings, but he couldn't any longer. She had been the same person down to her precise daily routine, but something was changing in Matt.

He heard the click, click, click of Sarah's heels, and he knew that she was waiting for him to get dressed. They had fought, and she had locked him out of the bedroom, and Matt had slept on the couch until Sarah came out to exercise. His head pounded when he heard the yelling voices of her video exercise instructors. Now Matt wanted to lay in bed and let the hangover wear off, but Sarah would be going to work and she never let him stay in her apartment when she left for the day.

Sarah let him kiss her on the cheek and he left. Matt remembered his reinstated credit card that Bill Ruby had returned to him last night, and he splurged on an Uber because his head couldn't deal with the subway today. Matt lived in a small two-bedroom apartment on the lower east side. It was more than he could afford. He'd had a roommate, but when his year on the sublet of the second bedroom had expired, his roommate was forced to move out. Sarah was his new girlfriend and she didn't like Matt having a roommate.

Matt knew now it had been a mistake. She'd only come over about five times, preferring that Matt always meet her at her luxury apartment. It didn't bother Matt because she was living the lifestyle he had intended to live, but he could have used a roommate to pay half of the rent.

Matt had worked less and less over the year. Years ago he had given up his early dreams of being a travel journalist for the draw of New York. He'd worked for magazines the last few years, but he just couldn't get inspired to interview celebrities anymore. Most of his freelance contacts had dried up because he'd said 'no' to opportunity too many times, but he couldn't say no to Charley. The Bill Ruby story could be a big payday for Matt in cash and contacts, and collateral with the future father-in-law.

When he got home, he sat on the couch and looked at the wall for three hours. Deep depression had rolled over him on the ride home, and it scared Matt because it had never happened before. He had always had a plan. He always knew where his life was taking him, but thinking about it, he realized that he hadn't written or sold an article in six months, and he couldn't find the old spark within himself. He hadn't written even one word on Bill Ruby, and though it might be career suicide, he had no intention of doing it.

Matt actually felt like crying. He didn't know where his life was taking him, and he had no aim anymore. He let his thoughts take him where they would and tried to meditate on his future, but there was nothing. He ignored his cell phone and he ignored the television. After three hours, Matt tried to picture himself as an old man, even older than his father was, and he tried to figure out what kind of life he would have by the time he was that age. That only made him think of his father who was a stand up world-class businessman, but there was no emotion there. Matt needed to feel energy in his work, and he couldn't keep doing a job day in and day out. He needed a spark, and that made him think of the crazy flash of white light that had come upon Reynolds and him.

Reynolds had been so infuriating, confronting him like that last night, but she had looked beautiful in that yellow dress. He couldn't believe that he hadn't even recognized her. She'd made him so mad at one point that he'd wanted to slap that smug smile right off of her face. There was no way he would write an article about Bill Ruby because he hated Bill Ruby.

He felt the pang of guilt that had been coming over him when he remembered the faces of the three boys. He hadn't seen them in weeks after only being with them for a couple of hours, yet he couldn't get their faces out of his mind. The oldest boy, William, looked exactly how Matt had looked in middle school. Matt let the depression wash through him, unable to reconcile that he might actually have three sons.

It was unfathomable, yet Reynolds had accepted it. Matt touched his shoulder and felt the sore spot. He was sure Reynolds would show up with the results at any moment, and he was positive that the results would be positive.

Matt moved to his desk and opened a document on his laptop that he hadn't opened in three years. It was the book that he told people he was working on, and he had it half written before giving up. This was the answer he had found at the edge of his angst-laden hangover, and as the day passed away, Matt plucked at the keys as though his life depended on it.

MATT TYPED FRANTICALLY, words spilling from his mind faster than he could type them. He hadn't even started the Bill Ruby article yet, but he'd already written more of his novel in the last six hours than he'd written in three years. He didn't want to think about where the inspiration was coming from, but it felt good. Like a bull rider, he'd opened the gate and was now holding on for dear life. The ideas came in waves and he tried to funnel them into coherent thoughts for the page.

You can't earn happiness in dollars so be true to yourself, Matt thought. It was something his mother had said to him since he could remember.

He cringed for a moment thinking again about the article he was supposed to be working on, and then he lost all steam when there was a knock at the door. Matt was shocked to see his father standing at the threshold.

"Dad," Matt said.

"Are you going to invite me in?" his dad asked, and Matt stepped aside and let him into the apartment. His father walked the space of the living room and then moved to the small dining table that doubled as Matt's office. Matt cringed as his father read the page that was open on the screen. He didn't want anyone to read his work right now, especially his father, but he didn't want to make a big deal about it.

Matt was always defensive around his dad and when his dad started to rub his chin, Matt knew something was wrong. It was his tell that he was stressed, and he'd come here to see Matt. His father had never made a visit unannounced, and since Matt had graduated college, he'd never visited without Matt's mother.

Matt wondered if his dad was going to try to get him into corporate banking again. Matt had attended college for finance, and to his father's utter dismay, Matt hadn't gone into corporate banking or worked his way up the ladder like he had. His dad was a self-made man, and Matt always felt that he could see the disappointment in his dad's eyes.

"How are you, son?" his dad asked, turning his attention to Matt but still rubbing his chin.

"I'm fine," Matt answered.

"Hmmm," his dad said, looking at the ground and starting to pace.

"You haven't called your mother."

"Is Mom okay?" Matt asked. Matt's mom had always had a soft spot for her boy, and she had defended Matt's decision to go into journalism out of college.

"She's fine. She's fine," his dad repeated himself.

The pit in Matt's stomach widened, and he thought his dad might be having a medical issue that he'd come to tell Matt about.

"So, you're fine, and there's nothing that you should be telling me or your mom?" his dad asked, and Matt turned white. He instantly thought of the trip to Ruby Island and the three mysterious boys who had materialized out of thin air, but there was no way Matt was going to tell his father.

"Sarah and I haven't set a date, if that's what you mean," Matt said trying to play it cool, but he was sweating now.

His father's face lost its composure and Matt saw a look he hadn't seen since he was twenty-three. His father was struggling for words, or he knew what he wanted to say, but it hurt him to say the words. There was anger and disappointment there, and his father had seemed to age twenty years since he'd come through the front door.

His father gulped back his indecision, and he squared up to Matt and looked him straight in the eye. "Matt, I saw the boys. The eldest, William, he is your spitting image."

Matt was shocked and angry at the same time. He couldn't believe that Reynolds would stoop so low as to call his father, and Matt could strangle her right now.

"Dad, you should stay out of this," he said, trying and failing to keep calm.

"No," his father snapped back and then took a deep breath.

"I don't know what Reynolds told you, but you don't know what's going on."

"I don't know any Reynolds," his dad said, and Matt was confused.

"I got a call from William. He's a smart boy. He found me on the Internet."

"William's on the Internet?" Matt asked worrying about the kind of trouble a pre-teen boy could get into on the Internet after spending a sheltered life stranded on an island. Matt shook his head.

"He found my phone number and left a message from a boy named William who said he was looking for his dad."

Deny, deny, deny, Matt told himself. "Dad, I don't even want kids and you're going to believe some stranger who leaves you a message? Really, you can't believe everything you hear. Get it together." Matt held his breath after he'd said that because he never talked back to his father. He was raised in a strict household, and flippant disrespect wasn't tolerated. He waited for his father's blowback, but it didn't come.

"I called the boy back and we had a nice chat," he said, and then he stared at Matt.

Matt was trying his best not to run out of the apartment. He wrung his hands together and stood stock still as his father paced some more.

"Let me tell you something, Matt. You're my son, and I love you." His father gulped again and Matt knew it was tears. They were not a very expressive family, and yet his father was having a hard time keeping it together. "I'm not telling you that you have to be with this woman, Matt, but if those are your boys, and they are," he said with certainty, "I will be very disappointed in you, ashamed of you, if you don't own up to being their father."

"Dad, they aren't my boys. I don't know what happened on that airplane. I mean, Reynolds is cute and all, but I don't even like her that way. I'm not interested in her like that." Matt wasn't sure why he'd said it like Reynolds was repulsive or something.

She was a knockout in the yellow dress. He shook his head and tried to focus.

His dad was staring at him, and Matt was more resolved than ever. He had no idea what had happened on that airplane, but there was no way that he had children. He felt panic, and he could see his future plans slipping away.

"Listen, son, I don't know what happened either. This is some miracle."

"Some miracle," Matt muttered, losing his fight.

His dad kept the stare for a moment longer before stepping closer and patting Matt on the shoulder. His dad clearly wasn't done yet, so Matt slumped into a chair and his father perched softly on the couch opposite Matt.

"Matt, William explained how you and Amy can't remember anything, and I don't know everything that happened, but I'm a grandfather, and you need to tell your mother because she needs to know. This changes everything."

"You're telling me," Matt said under his breath. He'd been denying, ignoring, and defensive when it came to mention of the boys, and he wanted to go about his life as it had been before the stupid flight to Ruby Island, but he was finally realizing that was impossible. Matt's father was forcing the issue, and he wouldn't let it go, not ever.

"And I didn't even get to take my grandsons to their first Yankees game," his father said with regret.

Matt nodded, and then realized what his dad had just said. "Wait, what?"

"Bill Ruby took them to the game yesterday."

"You're kidding," Matt said, his face reddening with anger. Bill Ruby was everywhere.

"You're a reporter and you don't know? There were pictures in all the papers. It was on the morning news, son."

Matt shook his head. "I'm not a reporter."

"You say that as though you're offended. Isn't your fiancé a reporter?" His dad smiled evenly, and Matt grit his teeth.

"She's a news anchor, not a reporter."

"You say tomato," his dad said.

"What's your point?" Matt said loudly. He hated when his father took an interest in his life. It usually meant he had some explaining to do, and Matt was too old for that.

"Sarah has a reputation to keep," Matt's father said as he rubbed his chin. He'd been charmed by Sarah for a long time, and Matt was beginning to think that his father no longer approved of her. It was one thing if Matt was getting tired of her, but that was a normal relationship hurdle. All of Matt's married friends told him the honeymoon would end someday.

"You don't like Sarah now?"

"She's fine, Matt. I like her just fine. It's more than that, son. Sarah is beautiful, and successful, and everything a man who tries to make it in this city wants. Heck, half of America is in love with her."

Matt nodded in agreement, and he sat a little higher in his chair. Sarah was all of that and more. She had access to New York City and soon the whole country, and she was on his arm. He'd gone to more red carpet parties and outrageously decadent fundraisers in the last year than he had in his life.

He'd been in green rooms before meeting Sarah, and he'd tagged along with a few celebrities while writing articles about them, but he'd never really felt part of that world. Sarah was glamorous, and Matt was hardly going to apologize for wanting to be with a beautiful woman at the top of her game.

"When I met your mother," his dad started, and Matt couldn't help but roll his eyes. Matt had heard enough "back when" stories from his grandfather to last a lifetime, and now he heard his grandfather's voice in his head telling him to show his father some respect. Matt cleared his throat but he didn't interrupt.

"When I met your mother, I didn't know right away that she was the one, but it didn't take too many dates to realize it. I didn't have much back then, Matt. I'd come to New York City with aspirations of building a business of my own, but it was expensive even back then. I worked as many hours as I could, but banking hours were pretty set, so it was hard to earn more at the time."

Matt was surprised to hear this. His father had always worked countless hours as the Chief Finance Officer on the 82nd floor of the company's building, and Matt had never thought of his father working his way up the ranks or struggling in any way. This was an eye opener.

"I spent most of what I had extra each month to take your mother out, and when I was ready to ask her to marry me, I had no money for a ring."

Matt had no idea where his father was going with this conversation. He guessed that seeing those boys had really rattled his cage. "That's too bad, Dad, but it all worked out in the end, right?"

"Matt, I sold everything I had to buy an engagement ring for your mom. I sold the luggage that my parents had bought me when I moved to New York, I sold most of the furniture I had collected in my apartment, and I even sold the gold plated pen that the bank had awarded me when I earned employee of the year." His dad looked at Matt and rubbed his hand over his chin.

Matt let out a sigh. Where was his dad going with this story?

"Matt, I was so in love with your mother that I had to marry her. I didn't care what things I had to let go of to propose to her the right way and to make sure she married me. That's how strongly I felt for her."

"Ha!" Matt blurted. "Have you seen the rock I put on Sarah's hand?" he asked his dad with a laugh. He was still paying that debt, but it was the ring that Sarah wanted and so he had to get it.

Matt's father nodded slowly and Matt could see that he was

trying to exert some patience with his son. Matt felt like a schoolboy who'd not done well on his report card again.

"Matt," his father said like a fifth grade teacher who was trying to get his student's attention, "I'm not specifically talking about the ring that I bought for your mother. I'm talking about how I felt when I sold everything I owned to buy it. I was in love, and I wouldn't let your mother go for the world. There was no other life for me, Matt, and if that's the way that you truly feel for Sarah, then I wish you the best."

Matt's eyebrows crinkled low on his forehead and a gnawing feeling returned the lump to his throat. Why was everyone trying to shake his confidence?

His father rose and dropped an envelope on the coffee table between them and Matt stared at it as his father walked to the door. "Go see those boys with an open mind, Matt, and you will see what I see."

att leaned forward to grab the envelope that his dad had dropped on the table, and he opened it. It was a picture of the oldest boy William, only it wasn't really him. It was Matt's own eighth grade picture. He jumped off the couch barely believing it was true. He'd noticed a resemblance, but he saw in this old photo that William was his spitting image, and now he understood his dad's demeanor.

Matt was more confused than ever. He'd been denying their very existence, and yet here was undeniable proof that the boys had to belong to him. Matt had been so focused on what he wanted that he hadn't stopped to think about his parents. He knew that his mom would be thrilled to have grandchildren, and he didn't need to give his dad another reason to be disappointed.

The walls felt like they were closing in, and Matt grabbed his keys and ran outside. He couldn't think straight. He couldn't breathe. He pulled out his cell phone and ordered a car to Reynolds' house, but when they were close to her brownstone, he changed his mind and now found himself in the elevator up to the 73rd floor of One World Trade Center. His mouth was dry when the doors opened, and Matt lumbered out into the lobby of the magazine office.

"Hi, Matt!" Danielle said from behind the desk. He waved and tried to smile, but his lip stuck to his teeth and he was sure it looked more like a grimace. He pushed the glass door open and felt his body shrink in on itself when he saw Sarah's face planted on half of the TV's that were mounted around the open expanse of the cubicle office.

It was so strange to wake up in her bed just this morning, and now he didn't know how he was supposed to feel about her. He was sure that they were just in one of their spats, and yet his father was right that she did have a reputation to uphold, and Matt owed it to her to say something about the kids. He looked over the sea of cubicles and saw Charley in his office and ducked lower wondering why he had come here.

"Mattey-Cole, Mattey-Cole, Mattey-Cole-Cole-Cole," he heard from Nicole's sing-song voice. He practically ran down the row to her cubicle to get her to quiet down.

"Nickey-cole," he said back playfully and tried to smile. He slinked into the larger than usual cubicle space and slipped into a chair. His eyes bulged at the photos hanging all around her and laying haphazardly on the desk.

There were newer photos of Reynolds with Bill Ruby at the gala mixed in with red carpet photos from the Oscars and the Golden Globes. He was shocked to see so many photos of Reynolds in elegant dresses.

"Is your mouth hanging open?" Nicole asked.

Matt snapped his mouth shut. "No!"

"She cleans up nice, doesn't she?" Nicole said, appreciating the photos again.

"I had no idea," Matt said.

"Mmm-hmmm," she said with a cluck of her tongue.

"I meant that I didn't know she used to date Bill Ruby."

"You didn't see this in your research?"

Matt crunched his teeth together. "I don't do research in advance. I find it taints my interviews."

"Mmm-hmmm," she said again.

That was most people's reactions when he told them he didn't do formal research before an interview. Sarah had said that it just made him unprepared and a bit of a snob.

"She's too down to earth for that lifestyle," Matt said.

"You're so blind. I can't believe she had a crush on you," Nicole blurted, and then she tried to cover her tracks. "Forget I said that."

"Who had a crush on me? Reynolds?"

Nicole shook her head. "You know, for one of the smartest men I know, you are really one of the dumbest men I know."

Matt stared at Nicole with his mouth open. There was no way that Amy Reynolds ever had a crush on him. He knew, in fact, that she hated him at this very moment.

"Remember those three in a row last year?"

"What, the back-to-backs you sent us on in the freezing Arctic winter weather? I have no idea what you mean." Remembering the frozen tundra, Matt's shoulders climbed up his neck as his body involuntarily shivered. It had been interesting to meet the Inuit people, and Reynolds had taken some fantastic photos. He had one printed of himself hanging in his apartment. It was just the circle of the parka opening, his wind chapped red face and five o'clock shadow a stark contrast to the blinding white landscape. They'd been trapped with the Inuit's for five days, and it wasn't even a terrible time.

"I sent you there hoping you'd get stuck for a while, and you did. You managed to get trapped in an actual igloo sitting around a fire in the frozen tundra, and you didn't even move in for a kiss!"

Matt grunted. What was Nicole even talking about? Reynolds was cute and all, and by these photos and how she looked in her dress at the fundraiser, even beautiful, but she'd never even hinted that she was interested.

"We were on assignment, Nicole. I'm a professional," Matt offered defensively.

She laughed. "Well, it all worked out because Amy's back with Bill and you are engaged to Miss Sarah Robinson, a.k.a. the boss' daughter." She winked at Matt.

"I don't know if we're close enough for you to make a joke like that," Matt said dryly. His head was spinning.

"I'm assuming you're here to turn in your article on Bill Ruby."

Matt shook his head, suddenly perturbed. "I'm here to see Charley," he lied. He rubbed his eyes and considered why he'd come.

"Hmmm," she said again.

"I need to see something from you, Matt. I'm an editor, I need something to edit, and your deadline is approaching."

"I didn't bring my laptop," Matt said. It was true, and he couldn't very well tell her that he hadn't written a word.

Matt's ears burned. He didn't know what to say about Bill Ruby, and seeing all of these photos of Reynolds with Ruby started to make him angry.

Those boys, those three boys that were going to ruin his life, they were the real article. And Reynolds, ambushing him with a DNA test - that was the real article.

Reynolds had a crush on me a year ago? Matt thought. Things were getting stranger by the minute.

Amy was sitting quietly in the kitchen drinking tea. It had been a while since she had sat alone without some interruption. She was starting to realize how exhausting three boys could be. All of her time seemed to be taken up now, and at least on Ruby Island the staff and the activities kept the boys busy. Here, they were always around her asking questions, or wanting her to read or watch TV with them or take them around the city. It was tiring, and it was a life she wasn't sure she would ever have, but now that it was reality, she liked it.

"It's exhausting having kids, isn't it?" Mabel asked, checking to see if the kettle had any hot water left in it.

Amy rubbed her forehead. "What would you know of it?" Mabel had already spent more time with the boys than she had when Amy was that age. Amy had always gotten along best with her father and she wasn't the proper beauty that she felt Mabel would have connected with better.

"What?" Mabel asked, filling the kettle and putting it on the stove. "We were always close."

Amy closed her eyes for a long moment and then opened them. She wanted to comment on the fact that by her mother's own request, she called her mother by her first name, but she left it alone. Now that Amy was quickly learning what it meant to be a mom, she could see that Mabel loved her in the best way that she could.

"It is exhausting. I can't help but think the boys would be better off on that island. They need so much activity."

"They're doing okay, and you couldn't have kept them there forever. Poor William has already hit puberty."

"Mabel," Amy complained.

"It's true."

"Knowing it and talking about it are two different things. Can we just leave that conversation alone?"

"Maybe his dad should have a talk with him," Mabel suggested, readying her tea bag and leaning against the counter to watch Amy's reaction.

"Maybe he should," Amy conceded.

"You know what we need?" Mabel asked, delicately brushing Amy's curly hair behind her ear. Amy reached up and held her mom's hand against her cheek, enjoying the touch. Benji and

Steven would lay down on the sofa and cuddle with Amy as they watched TV and Amy reveled in the warmth, but her mother Mabel rarely showed any physical affection, and it made Amy feel momentarily sad for her mother.

"What do we need?"

"Dinner out, just you and me. Go take a shower and get all gussied up, and I'll do the same."

"What about the boys?" Amy asked.

"Lucy can watch them," Mabel said in jest.

"I love her dearly, but Lucy doesn't watch her own boys."

"I'm joking. The boys will be okay. William is old enough to be in charge for a couple of hours."

Amy nodded her head. That was a better option than Lucy coming over any day. Amy jumped up and went to get ready, but Mabel remained in the kitchen and calmly made her tea because she had no intention of going to dinner.

my wondered why Mabel hadn't gone to change for dinner, but when she said to get a cocktail and wait for her at the table, Amy had been all too happy to comply. She could use a moment to decompress, and she enjoyed a slow walk in the perfect evening air. Mabel had made reservations. She liked the Milling Room for it's history as part of the luxurious Endicott Hotel. Where Amy took in the new decor, she knew her mother was remembering evenings she'd spent in the Palm Room under the arched glass roof back in the day.

Amy was shown to the table, and she ordered a drink and waited for Mabel. She took a sip of her appletini, and when she saw Matt Cole walk in, she almost spit it on the table. She hated her heart for skipping a beat, and she looked everywhere but toward the door. She needed to talk to him for weeks, but now was not the time. Matt Cole was engaged to be married and he was gorgeous, wonderful, and a jerk.

"Is this seat taken?"

"Not yet," Amy forced as she looked up at Matt. She was trying to keep her emotions tied up, but that just caused her cheeks to flood and she felt sweat on her neck. She guzzled the rest of her martini, which was a mistake because she didn't drink hard liquor that often.

Matt sat down and cleared his throat. He looked handsome in his white and blue button up shirt and fashionable jacket. The waiter passed by and Amy held up her glass signaling another drink. She closed her eyes and shook her head feeling the burn of the alcohol in her stomach. Amy could strangle Mabel right now.

They looked at each other for a moment, neither knowing what to say.

Finally Matt broke the silence. "I'm meeting my dad here for dinner. I don't know why I agreed to come, really." He shook his head.

"I thought you got along okay with your father," Amy said.

Matt fidgeted with the silverware. "I do."

The waiter put a fresh drink down and Amy took a quick sip of her second appletini. She didn't drink very often, but this dinner would need a little softening around the edges. *Mabel, what did you do?* Amy thought.

"Would you like something to drink?" the waiter asked.

"No, I don't think so. I'm not here with her. I mean, I'm not at this table," Matt stuttered.

"All evidence to the contrary," the waiter said with a smile.

"Go ahead, Matt," Amy said, her body flushing with embarrassment. They had been tricked into meeting for dinner. Their parents had somehow put them here together tonight, she was sure of it.

"I'll have a Jackie Gleason," Matt said, and the waiter nodded and turned on his heels to fetch Matt's drink.

"That sounds interesting," Amy said, not knowing what a Jackie Gleason consisted of.

"It's not really," Matt said, and he wiped his palms on his pants and then looked around the room for his father.

"So, is your dad late?" Amy asked.

"No," Matt said, tipping back in his chair to see if his father was seated on the other side of a half-brick wall. "Actually, I'm a bit late and I can't believe he's not here yet."

"It's a setup. He's not coming," Amy said.

"What?" Matt barked, automatically ready to accuse Amy for setting this up.

Amy put her hand up. "Hold on, Matt. It wasn't me. It was our parents. I'm supposed to be meeting Mabel here, and she's late too."

As if on cue, the waiter put a short glass of alcohol next to Matt, and both he and Amy guzzled down their drinks.

"Another round, garçon," Matt said. Amy could see his teeth clenching, and he reached up and rubbed his arm at the shoulder.

SOMEWHERE BETWEEN THE appetizer and main course, they were both able to relax as they returned to their typical banter. They had always worked well together and gotten along in their own way. Matt wanted to ask Reynolds if she'd really had a crush on him, but he just couldn't bring himself to do it.

"So are the boys officially Yankees fans?" he asked, trying to keep his cool about the game she'd let Bill Ruby take them to.

"Apparently thanks to you, they were fans before they even left the island," she said and then took a too large bite. "The first island," she clarified.

"You have something on your face," Matt said to Reynolds.

"It's my face, deal with it," she quipped back without raising her napkin.

"Really, it's on your cheek," he said, and she clowned around for a minute clearly one too many martinis into the evening.

"I can't believe that I cheated on Sarah with you," Matt said jokingly.

"Gee, thanks," she said, and she didn't look up at him. Matt wondered if Nicole was right and Reynolds had crushed on him.

"Well, I guess we were stranded for a long time on that island," he clarified.

"Stop while you're ahead," Amy jested. "I mean, I passed the 'if you were stranded on a deserted island with me' test."

"Don't sell yourself short, Reynolds. You passed the test at least three times."

"So you're ready to talk about the boys then?" she asked, turning serious. He had no idea how to respond. Seeing his own eighth grade picture and knowing it was the spitting image of the oldest boy, and his father's own reaction to the boys all clouded his ability to keep denying. His future had changed because somehow his past had changed.

Matt sat in silence as Reynolds continued. "I can't explain it either, Matt, but those boys are ours. I've really gotten to know them in the last few weeks, and I can't imagine life without them. Benji is sweet and everything excites him. And Steven is so smart and he contemplates every new thing he comes in contact with." She smiled. "I think he gets that overthinking thing from me. And William reminds me of you, and I can see your influence in him."

There was a pure soft joy on Reynolds' face as she talked about the boys, and it made Matt less afraid of the possibility.

"Reynolds, you're one of a kind," Matt said sincerely and she blushed.

"It's the Jackie Gleason's talking," she said, and they both laughed.

"Still, there's something about you," Matt said, leaning in and staring into her eyes. Could he see himself in a relationship with Reynolds? Before today it seemed far-fetched, but maybe there was something to it.

She looked right back and held his gaze for a moment, and then the truth of the situation seemed to rush over her because she was suddenly angry.

"Well, there is something about me. I'm the mother of your

children," she snapped and in that second Matt knew that the spell was broken. "Are you and Sarah going to have kids?"

"Honestly, we never talked about it."

"You're going to marry someone, and you don't even know what she wants for her future? Good plan, Matt. Real grown up." Amy threw her napkin on the table as she stood and just like that, she stormed out of the restaurant.

Matt tipped his head forward and rubbed his eyes hard. He took a deep breath and slugging down the last of his drink, he watched her go. She was right of course. He didn't plan anything, and the plans he made were rarely followed through. But the fact that she'd said it out loud made him angry enough to quickly pay the tab and follow her outside.

"REYNOLDS!" he called which made Amy walk faster. She regretted treating Matt like that, but she didn't know how to behave anymore. She could hear the tap of his shoes as he ran after her.

"Wait," he said and he grabbed her wrist and turned her toward him.

"What do you want?" she asked with as much fury as she could muster, but just knowing he'd come after her was enough to soften her anger.

"Just wait a minute," he said. Amy turned and kept walking, and Matt stayed in step with her, but he didn't take his hand off of her wrist. "I don't follow through with anything, you're right. I never have."

"You follow through, Matt. I was just... I don't know," Amy admitted. "You finished school and you became a journalist instead of a banker. You do follow through."

"Not with the important stuff," he said, pulling on her wrist so she would have to stop walking.

"What are you telling me, Matt?" Amy asked. She didn't know what she wanted him to say anymore.

"I don't know, Reynolds. I used to know. Damn, I used to be confident about everything I did and everything I thought."

Amy's anger subsided in his honesty. She had always loved his easy confidence and wondered from where he drew it.

"What is it, Matt? I'm tired of arguing. Why did you follow me?"

"Nicole said you had a crush on me," he blurted, and Amy's mouth dropped open. She could kill Nicole right now.

"She said that I had a crush on you? What, are we in high school now?" Amy tried to retort in anger but she was flustered, and it came out squeaky. She was two doors down from her mom's townhouse, and she wanted to go in and see the boys, but she was a little drunk and she should probably go straight to bed so they wouldn't see her drooling on herself.

"Did you?"

"Matt, I have three sons with you. I think I'm a little beyond crush at this point." She was being flip, but for some reason the truth gripped him in that moment, and he stepped in and kissed her hard on the mouth.

Amy was startled at first but she regained herself quickly, and it was a while before either of them pulled away.

"That didn't feel like a first kiss," Matt said. It was all so familiar and a bit shocking, and he resisted the urge to kiss Reynolds again.

"Make up your mind, Matt Cole," Amy said, and she turned and went up the stairs.

CHAPTER 15

When Amy woke up, she was still incensed at Matt for confusing her and at Mabel for setting the whole thing up. She was hung over from her too many appletinis, and she reached for her bottle of water and drained what was left of it. She sat up and groaned at the photos of her and Matt strewn across the floor around the bed.

He'd kissed her and she'd walked away hoping he would once again chase her, but she stood inside the door for a full five minutes, and he never knocked. He probably shook it off and went back to Sarah.

Amy took another lingering look at the images and the same lump formed in her throat. They'd had something real while stranded on that island, she could see it on her face in the photos, and she could account for it in the three wonderful boys they had raised together. She tried once again to remember, but she just couldn't pull any memories together.

She picked up the pictures and noticed one with her and Bill in the mix. The photo made something in Amy want to finalize anything that she and Matt had in common so she could start over with a clean slate. Bill was a great guy, and the boys really liked him, and plenty of kids grew up without their real fathers. The problem was that the boys had their father in their lives every minute up until Ruby Island, and she could see the toll that his absence was taking on them.

Amy moved to the side desk and powered up her computer. The only piece of business that she had left with Matt as far as she was concerned was the magazine article on Bill Ruby. She had the proofs of her shots ready to turn in, but Matt had admitted to her at dinner that he hadn't even started to write the article. He'd been sincere and even a little vulnerable when he'd told her that what had happened at Ruby Island had completely thrown him off guard. Amy was ready to put all that behind her and move forward with her life. She couldn't wait for Matt to grow up, so she decided that she would write the article.

Amy printed the article and emailed herself a copy to turn in to Nicole at the office. Just then Benji ran in and hugged Amy.

"Mama, you have to hear the bedtime story that Auntie Mabel told me." Mabel followed him in.

"You tell bedtime stories now?" Amy asked.

She winked at Amy. "It's the same story I've always told. Don't be jealous," Mabel said with a smile, and Amy gave her a deadpan stare. The 'same bedtime story' was Mabel not really telling a story at all.

"So how did this story go?" Amy asked Benji.

"Well, Auntie Mabel told me to try to guess what she was thinking, and I did! There was this giant air ship and the pilot was an iguana," he started, and Mabel giggled. Amy tried to listen attentively to Benji's fantastic tale, but her childhood of telling herself her own bedtime stories because she had "guessed" what her mother was thinking flashed before her. Mabel was now giggling uncontrollably, and she had to leave the room.

On her way out she told Amy, "The kid's a natural. You must have told him my bedtime stories on the island."

"Not funny, Mom. How would you like them to start calling you Grandma?" Amy asked, and Mabel popped back in the room.

"Don't you dare."

"Then don't you dare set me up on a date again... I mean dinner," she said, catching herself in front of Benji.

"I wanted to ask how that went, but I didn't want to intrude," Mabel said with a sly smile.

"Don't ask," Amy said. Giving Benji a squeeze and tickling him until he couldn't catch his breath. "Can you watch the boys for a bit? I need to run to the office and turn in the proofs for the article."

AMY MARVELED as the sun gleamed off of One World Trade Center. She never tired of hearing the sound of water falling in the 9/11 Memorial as she walked by on her way into the skyscraper. She was only twelve years old on that tragic day, and she'd never fully comprehended other people's loss. But at so many memorials, Amy had looked at people's faces through the lens of her camera. She could feel their utter loss as they stood and reflected.

Amy had come to the office partly because she needed to get out of the house and partly because she needed to turn in her photos to Nicole.

"Hold the elevator!" Amy heard, and she stuck her arm in the door to make it reopen.

"Thank you," Gary said with a wide smile, and Amy couldn't help but smile back. Amy hugged Bill's cousin. She would have been surprised to run into any friend or family on the elevator up to her office at One World Trade Center, but Gary always had that way of showing up where you didn't expect him.

"I heard you were in town," she told him, with a punch to his arm.

"Is Bill chatting me up again?" he joked.

"Actually, Matt Cole had many expletives to share with me about you."

"He's charming, Amy. I can see the draw for you. I mean, stranded on an island and all."

"Well, I must like Ruby Island better. I mean, especially since I can remember my time there."

"That's my girl."

Amy cleared her throat and closed her eyes for a long second. Gary loved his cousin, Bill, and he would do anything for him, but sometimes he pushed a little too hard. "Gary, you don't have to sell me on Bill. He's as wonderful as always, and the boys love to spend time with him."

"He loves you guys, too. He really wants to make a go of it," Gary said. Amy wanted to be irritated with Gary, but his beautiful blond locks and gorgeously tanned smile melted everyone, and she wasn't impervious.

"Maybe it is time for him to settle down then."

"That's what I just said to you," Gary said with another dashing smile. The elevator stopped at her floor and he followed Amy off the elevator.

"I can't believe that Bill would ask you to come and plead his case."

"Pardon me, Amy. Bill didn't ask me to say anything, but I want him to be happy, so maybe I overstepped. It's just that you looked like you were having fun at dinner, and I wanted to make sure you and Bill were on the same page."

Amy moved away from the elevator to the corner of the lobby that was furthest from the reception desk. She didn't want to believe that Gary was spying on her, but she wasn't sure if he was talking about dinner with Bill or Matt, and she didn't want to get into it.

"So if Bill didn't ask you to say anything to me, why are you here?"

Gary pulled a small envelope out of an inside pocket on his designer sweat suit. "I came to deliver the paternity test results. I think we both know what they say, but I wanted you to have a copy."

"Thanks," Amy said. She was blushing, and she knew Gary could see it on her face. She wanted to look at the envelope now but she slipped it in her bag. She instinctively looked around like she was doing something wrong, and she noticed Nicole standing in front of the plate glass window into the news room. Gary looked too and shot a smile at Nicole, and Amy watched her friend flutter in the window.

Amy moved to the elevator and pressed the down button. "Thank you for the visit, Gary. And thank you for watching out for Bill. I care about him, you know."

"I know you do, Amy."

"It's complicated, Gary."

The elevator dinged. "Aren't you going to introduce me to your friend?" he asked as Nicole walked toward them.

"Not today," Amy said, and Gary winked at Nicole before he got onto the elevator.

"Nothing in life is really confusing if you realize that every decision is simply a yes or a no. It's binary, Amy, it's ones and zeros. Make a choice," he told her, and the elevator doors closed.

"Who was that?" Nicole broke in.

"That's Bill's cousin, Gary."

"You have to introduce us," Nicole said. "He's gorgeous."

"He's a heartbreaker."

"He can break my heart for a night or two," Nicole said with a snap.

Amy chuckled. "I'm sure he'd be delighted. I'll give you his number."

Maybe Gary was right and everything was binary.

CHAPTER 16

Amy followed Nicole to her oversized cubicle and sat down.

"Nicole!" she complained when she noticed all the photos of her and Bill pinned up on the walls.

"It's called research," Nicole said. "Matt was very surprised to see some of these photos. He didn't know that you used to date Bill Ruby." Amy blushed and dropped a yellow folder on the desk.

"No wonder no one wants to hire Matt anymore. He doesn't do any research and goes in blind." Nicole shook her head.

"It's called being impartial," Amy said and then crunched her face. Why was she still defending him?

"In my world it's called being unemployed," Nicole shot back.

"Matt will come through," Amy said as confidently as she could. She had intended to bring the article she'd written today on a thumb drive and pass it off as Matt's, but part of her still hoped he would turn in the article on his own.

"And I expect Matt will have the inside scoop, since you are back together with Bill Ruby."

"I am not!" Amy yelled and then looked around to make sure no one was listening.

Nicole pointed to the newspaper photo of Amy and Bill together at the gala dinner. "A picture says a thousand words."

Nicole opened the yellow folder that Amy had dropped on her desk. She perused the prints of the photos Amy had taken of Bill Ruby, nodding her head.

"Matt hasn't sent me anything to go along with these photos yet, not even an outline. It's not a good sign, Amy. I told you he'd lost his touch. His article better be good."

"He'll get you a story."

"He'd better. He hasn't worked much this year, not since he got engaged to Charley's daughter. He must think he can just ride it out now and he'll end up with a position at the magazine, but it's competitive here, and there's no way Charley is going to play the nepotism game."

Nicole's desk phone beeped and she looked at the Caller ID before picking it up. "Speak of the devil," she said to Amy and then pulled the receiver to her ear. "Yes?" she asked. Then she nodded and looked at Amy. "Yes, sir," she said and hung up.

"Charley wants to see you before you leave."

"Well, are we done here?" Amy asked. She usually liked to spend time with Nicole, but talking about Matt and Bill in the same conversation was exhausting.

"Not until you send me Gary's phone number," Nicole teased with a smile.

"I'll text you," Amy promised. "We're good on the photos for the article?"

"Yes, these are great," Nicole said looking over the prints again. "Very natural, Amy. Did you get Bill Ruby to jump off a waterfall and climb a tree to pluck coconuts for the photo shoot, or is that how you roll on Ruby Island?"

Amy loved the photos of Bill in his natural surroundings and with her boys, but she had omitted some of the best photos because she didn't want the kids in the article. "I guess you will have to try to date Gary for more than one night and maybe you will get to find out yourself.

"Girl, now you're talking! Do you want me to take the negatives to Sam? You're not the only dinosaur around here, and you know he'll love to see actual film negatives again." Nicole smiled at Amy who shook her head.

"Just keeping it real," Amy said, and she and Nicole snapped their fingers and pointed at each other. Amy strode over to the large glass windows that surrounded Charley's office and then she stopped in her tracks.

Charley was standing and looking out the windows over New York City. His trademark black suit that was always crisp and unwrinkled even after a full day's work was showing signs of wear. She could see that he had his arms crossed and his stillness signified someone deep in thought.

Amy looked on in dread. Everything about this scene was wrong. She shared a look with Charley's executive secretary who shrugged, giving Amy the wave to go right in.

"You rang," Amy said as she pushed Charley's office door open slowly. Charley spun around and smiled, but Amy could see the lines on his face, and she could tell that he'd lost sleep.

"Amy, how are you, my dear?"

Amy walked to the comfortable gray chair in front of Charley's desk and plopped down. "I'm fine," she said tentatively, but she didn't sound it. She tried to smile because the last thing she wanted to do was talk to Charley about her problems, and she was curious as to what what going on with him.

"Really?" he asked, sitting slowly in his chair and leaning forward.

Amy's heart sank. She could always talk to Charley, but not this time. "I'm fine. I'm really fine, Charley." She sat up straight and brushed her palms on her pants, looking into his eyes to try to guess what was bothering him. Charley was always on top of his game, but Amy could see more signs of wear in his eyes, and he had a five o'clock shadow before noon.

"So you're fine," he confirmed with a nod. "I'm so glad, because last time I saw you at the gala, you didn't look fine."

"You didn't like my dress?"

"Your dress?" Charley laughed. "Oh, it was really something, Amy. I've said before that you should be in the photos you take." Charley smiled sincerely, and in that moment, Amy missed her dad. Charley had been a friend for a long time, and his distinguished and gentlemanly demeanor always reminded her of her father.

"I was just concerned because you seemed to be arguing with Matt at the gala, and I could tell you were upset." He watched Amy for a reaction, and she almost jumped out of her chair. Charley only beat around the bush when he was playing cat to the mouse, and she didn't know what to say. There was no way Amy was going to admit the truth about Matt, not to his future father-in-law.

When Amy didn't answer, Charley leaned confidently back in his chair.

"How's your sister doing?" Charley asked, and Amy's eyes jerked from her fingernails to Charley's eyes.

"Charley, are you feeling okay? You know I'm an only child."

"That's right, that's right," he said dismissively. "I thought for a minute I was losing my mind though. When Mabel posted those photos on Facebook and said that she was with her grandsons, and how happy she was, I just about fell out of my chair."

"Mabel's on Facebook?" Amy asked incredulous. For all of her loquaciousness, her mother had abhorred the Internet revolution.

"Yes, she is. We don't keep in touch like we used to, but it's nice to catch up sometimes to see what she's up to. And would you look at that?" Charley said, pointing to his computer screen. Amy looked at the floor though, and her hand covered her eyes.

She sighed loudly as Charley turned his computer monitor out toward the front of his desk.

"There she is posing with three boys and it says, and I quote, 'Showing these three young men the town. They're my long lost grandsons!'"

Amy looked up and read the caption before cradling her face in her hands. She groaned and then laughed and then groaned again.

"So, if you're an only child, is there something you wanted to tell me?" Charley turned the monitor back toward his desk and sat back in his chair, ever patient.

"No?" Amy asked.

He leaned in toward his monitor and clicked his computer mouse a few times to zoom in. "Amy, the two younger boys look just like you."

"Well, we are all related to Mabel."

"And are they related to Matt?" Charley asked.

"What?" Amy squealed, clamping her hand to her mouth. She bit her lip and almost fell off the edge of her seat.

"Well, the oldest boy here looks just like a very young Matt Cole. And I saw you arguing with him the other night which was very strange. At first, I thought it was about the article, which he hasn't turned in, by the way." Charley looked at Amy and smiled.

"I just gave Nicole the photos, and I'm sure Matt will have the article to you any day now." Amy leaned forward to stand, but Charley shook his head and pointed at the chair.

"You stay right where you are, Amy. I have some questions for you," he said sternly, and Amy's face turned a deeper shade of red. She felt as though Charley's window office had turned into an aquarium and everyone outside was looking in. Her stomach churned.

"I said I'm fine, Charley. Can we leave it at that?" Amy suddenly felt like crying, but she laughed instead. "I mean, I have some things I have to take care of, but I'm fine. Really."

"I called Mabel to ask her about the boys," Charley told her.

Amy felt every cell in her body moving position, and she thought she might shed her skin right there on his office floor. "And?"

"And she said that I needed to talk to you."

Amy let out a long breath and bit her lip again.

"So, I called Bill Ruby. I wanted to thank him for taking such good care of you while you were sick on his island."

Amy nodded and covered her face with her hands. She'd seen Charley work his inquiring magic on so many others, and he'd done it to her at times. He could extract the truth from a pathological liar without them knowing he'd done it.

"I also asked Bill about you and Matt, and the three boys in the photo."

"Why would you do that?" Amy asked. "There's no proof of anything really."

"No proof. What do I need proof of?"

"So what did Bill say?" Amy caught herself and told herself to stop talking. She stared at Charley, but she needed to get out of this office if she was going to keep her secret. She wouldn't lie to her old friend, but she didn't want to tell him the truth either. Her three sons were also the three sons of the man who was engaged to Charley's daughter. It would be a lose-lose conversation.

"Bill said I would have to talk to you. So, Mabel and Bill both say I need to talk to you, and here I am doing just that."

Amy stood and walked to the window behind Charley's desk. She knew that everyone would find out sooner or later, but she thought it would be best that Matt tell Sarah first. She shook her head as all of her thoughts screamed out at one time.

"Little Dan Dougie says 'hi'," Charley said, and Amy grunted again. Little Dan Dougie worked wonders with a telephoto lens. He'd left the magazine for a life as paparazzi, and with the invention of digital magazines and TMZ, he'd made a killing taking indiscreet photos of celebrities. He also did the odd side job for Charley, under the table of course, since the magazine had a reputation to uphold.

"I don't want to see the photos," Amy said embarrassed that Little Dan might have clicked a picture of her and Matt kissing on the street. It would have been excruciating to look at that in front of Charley.

"It's so unbelievable, it's outrageous really," Amy said. "The Bermuda Triangle is the only way I can explain it. I want to talk to you, Charley, I really do, but I'm just coming to terms with it, and it's not only my story to tell."

Charley nodded and some years seemed to melt away from his face as she admitted there was some truth to be told. Amy knew that he would accept anything she told him as truth. She could tell him that aliens abducted her, and Charley would believe it because he trusted her.

Charley moved to the window and faced Amy.

"Anna Banana," he said gently, and some of Amy's tension fell off. "I won't try to understand how, and you will have to explain sooner than later, but do you somehow have children with Matt?" he asked.

"You shouldn't say that about your daughter's fiancé." When she looked up at Charley, she thought he understood her without words.

"My daughter, Sarah, is smart and beautiful and completely capable of getting what she wants in this world. If that's Matt, then I'm happy for her. I'm not worried about my daughter, Amy, not ever."

"I know," Amy said. "Sarah's always been an unstoppable force."

"However, if Matt happens to have children with another woman, let's say you perhaps, then I think you owe it to yourselves to do the research on the relationship and see if there is a future there. Call me old-fashioned, but you should try for the children's sake."

Amy had been crying, and she pulled the handkerchief out of his breast pocket and dried her tears before turning back toward the large office window. No one was watching, but she knew that at least Nicole was somewhere with eyes on the situation.

Amy patted Charley on the shoulder and went back to her chair to retrieve her bag. "What do you want me to say, Charley?" she asked.

"I want you to tell the truth, Amy. And if not to me, then tell it to yourself. You deserve to be happy. I don't know if that means Bill Ruby or someone else, but tell yourself the truth and you'll find happiness."

"What about Sarah?" Amy asked.

"Oh, I just hope I'm there to see Matt try to explain that one," he said with a smile.

"Charley, thanks for everything," Amy said with a sigh. "Please excuse me. I've got to go get Mabel to delete her Facebook account."

CHAPTER 17

Amy barely kept it together on the elevator down, whipping out her phone and trying to work the app to call for a ride. She'd been stranded on an island for thirteen years and had three beautiful boys with a man who was more and more like a stranger. It wasn't her fault that man was engaged to Charley's daughter. Amy was as much a victim in this as anyone, so why did she have to feel so guilty about the whole situation?

The elevator opened and she got out before she realized she wasn't at the lobby yet. Amy huffed at herself and crammed back on the elevator. She tried to clear her head, but Charley's words followed her down to the lobby and out the front door. Amy rounded the corner to where her ride was waiting, and as she was pulling the car handle, she heard a high pitched double-beep and looked up to see Bill Ruby pull up in his car.

Bill jumped from the small green Mini Cooper that he'd intended for William. "Need a ride, sexy?" he purred to Amy, and she almost dropped her phone.

"Bill, what are you doing here?" she asked, but she already knew that Gary had told him where to find her.

"You're Bill Ruby," Amy heard her driver say.

"Oh great," Amy whispered.

"Yes!" Bill said enthusiastically. He walked back to talk to the driver before he could get out of the car. "I'm here to give her a ride, but how about you follow us so that you don't lose the fare?"

"Sure! Can I get a photo with you first?"

"Of course," Bill said. He leaned down and took the guy's phone, turning to get himself and the driver in the shot while Amy tried not to come apart at the seams. She didn't want to see Bill right now, but it was pointless. She knew from experience that if she got into this guy's car, he would just question her about Bill Ruby the whole ride.

She moved up to the Mini but she waited for Bill to open her door because he was a gentleman to the hilt. It was charming on most days, except on days that Amy wanted to crawl into a dark hole.

"I'll try to keep up," Amy heard the driver say, and Bill laughed as he slid in next to her.

"Home to Mabel's?" Bill asked.

"Sure," Amy said, and in an instant he had shifted and they were rocketing down the street. Amy could see Bill looking in the mirror and she could tell that he was ready to have fun with the driver who was following. Amy knew that Bill could lose him if he tried, but he drove normally in the medium traffic of the late morning.

"Did Gary tell you that it's binary?" Amy asked sarcastically.

"No," Bill said patiently. "Were you and Gary discussing computer coding for some reason?"

Amy laughed because she wanted to cry, but she couldn't get into it with Bill right now. She needed some space alone, somewhere to think, but all she'd been doing for weeks is think and it wasn't getting her anywhere. The truth was unfolding and she couldn't stop it from happening.

"Bill, I'm pretty sure that the magazine has photos of you with the boys. I didn't give them any for the article, but they received some from a disreputable source."

Bill was silent, so Amy looked over at him as he smoothly turned the corner and shifted quickly, putting a few seconds between himself and the follow car. To her surprise, he was smiling.

"Amy, my photo was in the paper with the boys the day after the Yankees game. It's okay," he said, and he reached over and put his hand on hers. For a split second Amy felt as though she should take her hand away, but the familiar warmth of his strong hand was comforting, so she turned her palm up and held his hand until he needed it back to move the stick shift.

"Amy, I know you have a lot going on, and it's been a lot for you to adjust to, but if we're going to be together, there are going to be photos of the boys that get out."

"That get out?" Amy chirped. "They'll be stalked!" She regretted saying it like that, but it was true. Bill Ruby was known all over the world, and although she'd joked with him about his private island in the past, she thought she might have an inkling of understanding why he needed that space.

"That's something you will have to think about, too," Bill said with regret. He pulled over so he could look directly at Amy, and she melted a bit under his full gaze. He was fantastically put together and his chiseled everything drew her in like a moth to a flame.

"Amy, I think we can build something wonderful together. There is a reason you crashed on my island."

"We didn't crash. Matt landed the plane."

"Okay, whatever. What I'm saying is, let's do this. Let's give this a go, Amy. You know we are great together, and I love spending time with the boys too, and they like me. We can be a family. The sky is literally the limit with me. You know that. I'll take care of you and the boys, and I will protect you and the boys."

Amy was frustrated with herself for not falling into his arms that very second. He would take care of her and the boys, and his life could be her life. She would have estates to travel to and enjoy each year, and a staff to assist her with any need. The boys would go to great schools and she could be a stay-at-home mom for them. She would want for nothing.

Bill was looking into her eyes, and Amy could tell that he was truly sincere, and she knew that she should feel the same way. Still, there was something in her mind calling her away from Bill just as it had last time.

"I admit that the last time we dated you helped me through a really hard time when I lost my dad, and maybe that was part of the emotion there, but this is different, Amy. This is just you and me."

"And William and Steven and Benji."

"Of course, you know what I mean."

Amy felt so grateful in the moment and so drawn to Bill, and maybe Gary and Charley were right and she just needed to choose. She leaned in and kissed Bill on the lips and felt the familiar safety in his kiss. *His fans would not be disappointed,* Amy thought, as she pulled him closer. A minute passed and she leaned back and then she smiled. The driver who had been following them had pulled alongside and he was staring into the car. Amy laughed, breaking Bill's spell.

"I think he really wants me to take that ride," she said as she unbuckled. She took Bill's hand and looked straight into his eyes. "I heard you, Bill, I really did, and I will consider everything you said."

"Let's go spend some time back on the island, Amy. It will be good for the boys."

Amy nodded as she got out of the car. "That sounds wonderful," she said. "I'll talk to Mabel to make sure she can live without them for a little while. Call me tonight."

Bill winked and put the car in gear, speeding out between two cars that would have been too tight for anyone else to even try. *Bill Ruby, fearless and wonderful,* she thought as she got in the back seat of her waiting ride.

∾

When Bill drove away, Amy texted Lucy that she was coming over. She was losing her mind and needed to talk to her friend and confidant. When the door opened to the three-story town-house mansion, Amy smiled at the housekeeper and was led inside. It was strangely quiet as the housekeeper led Amy out the French doors in back to the brick terrace where Lucy was sitting and sipping lemonade.

Lucy stood and gave Amy a peck on each cheek and then turned seriously to the housekeeper who was waiting instruction. "Miss Kretz, you make sure the boys stay out of our way and also that this pitcher does not run out." They smiled tight smiles at each other and Miss Kretz nodded and turned to leave.

"She's new," Amy said as the housekeeper moved inside.

"She's wonderful. She's from Germany. She's very formal, and she's fair but strict with the boys."

"I see that," Amy said, impressed. "What happened to Veronica?"

"Oh, she's still the boys' nanny and tutor, but when Veronica isn't around, Miss Kretz has them set straight. It's wonderful. You might never see me with the boys outside this house again unless I can get Miss Kretz to chaperone them. That's why it's so quiet right now. The boys are hiding from her." Lucy chuckled and offered Amy a lemonade.

"Tell me it's spiked," Amy said, thinking of her own boys and taking a long drink from the cold glass.

"But of course," Lucy answered, refilling both glasses. "What's going on? You don't drink before noon."

Amy downed a second glass and tried not to lose it as she told

177

Lucy everything, from her dinner with Matt to her meeting with Charley to her kiss with Bill Ruby in the car just thirty minutes before.

"Wow, you get around girl," Lucy said, refilling Amy's glass, but Amy let it be for now.

"Lucy," Amy moaned, and Lucy chuckled.

"We both know you have never gotten around, Amy. That was me. How do you think I got all this?" Lucy spread her hands at the larger than usual and impeccably manicured New York City backyard.

"Well, if I remember correctly, you had what you thought would be a one night stand with a guy from the bar, who you fell in love with in about a day, and he turned out to design the next big app. And you thought you were slumming it."

"I know, right?" Lucy said. "Jackpot! Now what are we going to do about you?"

Amy leaned forward and put her face in her hands, mumbling through her fingers. "The boys are at home with Mabel, and I just don't know what to do next."

"You'll have to enroll them in school, or home school them if you think they aren't ready for the full immersion."

"Oh my God, I hadn't even thought about school." She felt the alcohol warm her and took a deep breath in. "I'm such a bad mother. I'm more worried about Matt and Bill than I am my own children."

"Well, you have a life too, my dear."

"Do I?" Amy asked. "What is it? Tell me what to do, Lucy."

"I will if you want me to. I think it's an easy decision, really."

"You do?"

"Of course, sweetheart. Let Bill get his way. Allow him to sweep you off your feet. The boys like him, and he has the means to take care of everything. You can't tell me that doesn't sound wonderful."

Amy bobbed her head as though she couldn't decide to agree

or disagree. "A month ago you were telling me to go for it with Matt. Now you think I should date Bill."

"A month ago, Matt was a catch and you were crazy about him. Now, Matt is a deadbeat dad who won't even acknowledge his sons' existence, and although he kissed you in the street, he hasn't called or followed up. While Bill is an ex-boyfriend who is still in love with you, likes your kids, and he wants to take care of you. What's the choice here, Amy? Your mind has been made up for you. Go with it!"

Amy blushed. Everything Lucy said was right and yet it was impossible to make up her mind. Choosing Bill Ruby meant letting go of her two-year crush on Matt, but she had to come to terms that the daydreaming was over and reality had her in a stranglehold. Even if the crazy miracle of their boys hadn't happened, Matt was engaged to Sarah Robinson, and he was off limits.

"You're thinking of Matt again, but that's a fairy tale and that ship has sailed," Lucy said softly.

"More like that plane has crashed." Amy gulped back tears and then clinked glasses with Lucy. "Thanks, lady. I knew I came here for a reason."

MATT COULDN'T STOP THINKING about the kiss with Reynolds. It was their first kiss, but it was so familiar. It had kept him up at night. Maybe they were really stranded together on that island, and maybe they had fallen in love. Matt didn't know what to believe anymore. He spent two days writing his book and thinking about Reynolds and ignoring Sarah's phone calls. His reverie ended with a knock at his front door.

It was Blondie again, the one who had stabbed a needle through his tuxedo jacket in the tailor shop, and Matt flinched involuntarily.

"G'day, mate," Gary said flashing a movie star smile.

"Is it?" Matt asked, ready to close the door.

"Sure, might be the best day of your life," the man said, and he slapped a large envelope into Matt's stomach. Matt grabbed the paper and before he could slam the door in the guy's face, Blondie had turned and gone.

It wasn't the best day of Matt's life, though. The envelope held the paternity tests for all three boys, and they were positive, depending on which side of the aisle you were standing. It was official; Matt was a father. He had already been coming to grips with this fact after seeing his own school photo and realizing the similarity between he and the older boy was uncanny.

Matt had heard of divine intervention before, but he wouldn't actually believe in it until he looked back on this moment some years later. As soon as he'd opened the envelope and saw the results, his doorbell rang and rang until he answered. It was Sarah at the very worst possible time.

"I will not be ignored, Matt," she said as she stormed by him into the apartment. Matt thought that it was strange to see her here since she had stopped spending time at his apartment, insisting that he come to hers instead.

When he closed the door and turned to her, she was standing with her arms crossed, tapping the toe of her high heel on the floor. She hated losing her cool, Matt knew, and his two-day hiatus must have been too much for her ego to bear.

"Where have you been?" she snarled.

Matt sighed heavily and played out several ways this conversation could go in his mind. He was riding a high and a low all at once. Writing his novel had been the best time he'd spent in years and he didn't know how to express that to his fiancé, but the insanity of his paternity, combined with the fact that Matt just didn't know if he was supposed to marry a girl like Sarah anymore, drew him down.

"I've been writing my novel, finally," Matt said with a smile.

"You're writing a novel?"

Matt's head jerked back. Had he never told Sarah that becoming a fiction writer was his dream in life? It wasn't possible.

"Well, yes, I'm writing a novel."

"Okay," Sarah said, and he could see that she was trying not to condescend to him, but that was tough for Sarah, especially when she felt indignant in her anger. "So you couldn't answer the phone?"

Matt cleared his throat. He could defend himself all day, but as much as he loved Sarah, there was only one tack to take.

"What do you think of having children?" Matt asked.

"Out of the question," Sarah retorted, turning to admire herself in the mirror on the dining room wall. Then she turned back to Matt. "I'm not saying never, I'm just saying maybe in a few years depending on how things go at the network. Is that's what's going on? You want children? Jesus, Matt, we're not even married yet."

He could see that she was about to really lose her temper, but he had to push on.

"How about stepchildren?" Matt asked.

"Are you telling me that you are going to have kids with someone else?"

Matt pulled out the paternity test and put it on the table. "I don't remember it, but apparently I already do."

Sarah snatched the paper from the table and read Matt's name along with "positive" and had seen enough. She threw the paper down. Matt watched her face for a reaction, and Sarah had pressed her lips tightly together. She was trying not to overreact, but Matt knew she was about to explode.

"So you have a son."

"I do," Matt said, glad that she hadn't flipped through the report to see that there were actually three sons. She would find out eventually, but he didn't want to rub salt in the wound just yet.

"And did this happen while we were together?"

"Not technically. He's over five years old."

Matt could see Sarah's shoulders relax once she was secure that he hadn't cheated on her. He was ready to explain the entire situation depending on her next move.

She looked over in the mirror again and then moved to the window, and Matt gave her space to mull it over.

"So, what do you think of being a stepmother?" he asked.

Sarah walked to Matt and took his hands. "Matt, sweetheart, do you believe in divine intervention?"

Matt shrugged.

"I'm not going to pretend to understand why this happened, but it did, and that's that." She smiled sweetly and Matt smiled back, surprised at her acceptance of the situation. Sarah ran her thumb over the dimple on Matt's chin and sighed.

"I have a career to think about, and things here just got way too complicated for me." Sarah pulled the large diamond engagement ring off her finger and held it out in front of her. "A memento," she said, slipping the ring into her pocket as she turned and walked out the door.

AMY WAS PACKING for the trip to Ruby Island when a messenger dropped off a large envelope late in the evening. She was surprised to see a manuscript from Matt inside. There was a note card that simply said, "Who says I'm not a writer? - Matt".

Amy put the boys to bed and couldn't help herself. She stayed up all night reading the thriller, and at four in the morning she finished. She was very happy for Matt who had finally finished his first novel. The story was fast-paced and exciting, and the characters had a surprising level of depth.

Amy felt a sense of finality in the work, and she found herself wiping away tears. She was taking the boys back to Ruby Island for an undetermined length of time. She'd told Bill that she needed time and space and he seemed to understand, and he'd invited her to go to the island to take as much time as she needed. He would begin shooting another sequel next week anyway and wouldn't be around, and that would give Amy the space she needed to figure things out.

Amy knew that she'd left Bill with an inkling of hope that they might have a future, but she felt in her heart that it wouldn't work out. She wasn't looking back anymore, and both Bill and Matt were in her past. She needed to focus on her three boys.

Amy made fresh coffee and then went to the desk in her dark room where she opened up her laptop and sent Nicole the article she'd written in Matt's name. She sent it with a note that Matt wanted Amy to fact check the article since she had a "thing" with Bill these days. She read over the email, and when she decided it sounded plausible, she hit send.

Nicole responded immediately with kudos to Matt for finishing the article, but Amy didn't respond. She didn't want Nicole or anyone knowing that she was going away, and she figured they'd hear about it because she was sure that Little Dan Dougie would find a way to get photos.

my had finished packing for herself and was waiting for the boys to wake up so she could get their things together. She was looking at the pictures from a lifetime she couldn't remember when William came in.

"Hi, mom," he said, and he walked around the counter to see what she was looking at. It was a picture of Matt and William at around Benji's age.

"Chucky," William said, pointing at the makeshift doll that he held.

"What?" Amy asked.

"You made me that doll and dad named it Chucky and you guys used to laugh about that."

"I made that?" Amy asked, leaning in to take stock of the doll. It was palm fronds and several bits of material from clothing with button eyes and a threaded smile. Amy had been horrid at crafting, and she couldn't believe that she had made the doll.

"You did a lot of things you don't remember," William said, moving to the next picture. Amy watched him as he took in the images, and she could see that he was enjoying the memories.

She'd seen that same smile on Matt's face and the likeness was undeniable.

"You and Dad used to talk to us sometimes about being stuck on that island. You both said that God made you crash there so that you could have the family you never would have. You said you were already in love with Dad, and he said he needed a big bump on the head to figure things out."

"I was in love with your dad," Amy said, truthfully.

"And he loves you, Mom, he just can't remember." Amy squeezed William on the shoulder. "Do you want me to hit him in the head?" he asked.

"Maybe," Amy laughed. "William, we're going to go back to Ruby Island for a while. Not with Bill, just you and me and your brothers. I think it's time we talked about how we want to live now that you made it back to the real world. I hope that's okay."

William nodded. "Can Auntie Mabel come?"

"Not this time," Amy said, because she had no intention of letting her mom anywhere near her getaway. "But I'm glad you like your grandmother, and we will come back soon. Call it an extended vacation."

"That's what you used to say on the island," William reminded her, but as hard as Amy tried, she couldn't remember.

AMY WAS SITTING in front of a large basket of Godiva chocolates that Mabel had bought for the boys. She was on her fourth piece when Mabel came into the kitchen and poured herself some coffee.

"This won't help your figure."

"It's helping my brain though," Amy replied as she put the last piece down on the table, clearly having eaten way too many chocolates.

"Mabel, I've decided to take the boys back to Ruby Island for a while."

"What about their father?"

"What about him? He hasn't been much of a father for the past month."

Mabel took a long sip of her coffee and sat down at the kitchen table. "It's a funny thing when you learn how to dance a dance. A woman learns all the steps to the dance, and a man learns all the steps to the same dance, but a woman innately knows not to put her foot down right away, even if she is certain of the steps. She learns to feel the man's movements, and react. You learn to follow him, and even though it's a millisecond difference, it's there."

"Mom," Amy said, hoping that would distract Mabel from whatever it was she was trying to say.

"You know what I mean, Amy. Even in a simple waltz with your father, you didn't put your toe on the ground until you were certain he'd taken his full step."

Amy thought about it, and Mabel was right about dancing.

Mabel looked at Amy and waited for her daughter to meet her eye. "Don't put your foot down yet, Amy. Just wait another second to commit your step. You never know what might happen."

"But Mabel, you're missing the whole point. Matt's not dancing with me. He's dancing with someone else completely."

"He's a good man, Amy. I've spent hours listening to the boys tell stories about growing up, and both you and Matt were wonderful parents. Give him some time to come around."

Amy watched a tear roll down Mabel's face and Mabel reached out and brushed Amy's curly bang behind her ear. "You know, your father would love these boys. He would treasure them as much as he treasured you," Mabel said wholeheartedly.

Amy smiled but her mom's show of emotion made her squirm. "Mom, stop that."

"That I love you makes you uncomfortable?"

"It's not that. It's just that you don't cry, for anything really." Mabel sniffled and wiped her face, giving Amy a squeeze on her arm.

"Well, I guess becoming a grandmother has caught me off guard."

"Oh, Mom," Amy said, smiling warmly. "Does that mean you are going to let the boys call you grandma?"

"Not on your life!"

They shared a smile and then Amy's phone pinged. She read the text from Nicole. *The article looks great and copy is going to have Matt make a couple of tweaks and we will be ready to print for next month. Thanks for the scoop. I'm meeting Gary for lunch and if all goes well you won't hear from me for a few days. Wink! Wink!*

Amy started to text back, but there was nothing she could say to explain the fact that she wrote the article. She just hoped that Matt wasn't stupid enough to admit that he hadn't written it.

CHAPTER 19

The copy editor had called Matt to say he was sending over a couple of edit ideas, and he needed the revised article back in a day.

"How did you get my article?" Matt asked incredulously as he stared at the blinking cursor. He'd written garbage, so he had never sent the article in. This article that had been emailed back sounded like him, but it wasn't his work.

"Nicole sent it over. It's the softer side of Bill Ruby, and it's great work, Matt. If you can fix the markups and get it back to me by tomorrow, we will be good to print."

Matt was silent as he ground his teeth. He started to re-read the article as his face turned red. This was good writing, and personal. Only someone close to Bill Ruby would be able to write this type of piece. Reynolds was close to Bill Ruby, and she was friends with Nicole. He knew that Reynolds had written it, and he wanted to punch something. Matt was both grateful and enraged.

"Uh, thanks," Matt stuttered. "Glad you like it. I'll get back to you by tomorrow then." Matt hung up and read the article three more times. He was wondering if he should make the edits and take credit for the article or strangle Reynolds, when the doorbell rang.

"You!" Matt yelled at Reynolds, and he turned back to the dining room, leaving the door open behind him.

AMY WENT INSIDE and closed the door, ready for the barrage of anger that was sure to come. She watched Matt pace for a minute.

"You are unbelievable!" Matt yelled.

"You're welcome!" Amy yelled back. She'd told herself the whole way over that she would stay calm and be rational, but seeing Matt made her so frustrated that she couldn't hold back.

"Welcome for what?"

"For giving you this job and for saving your ass," Amy blurted. "You've been floundering for a long time, Matt. You don't meet deadlines and your work isn't up to par."

"For giving me this job?"

Amy crossed her arms. "Did you meet the deadline for this article?"

"Well, no, but it's been a crazy month."

"I was able to spend time with three boys and write the article, Matt!" Amy yelled at the top of her lungs. He was so infuriating and she wanted to slap him.

"What do you mean that you gave me this job?" Matt yelled back just as loudly.

"I gave the story to the magazine as long as they put you on it, Matt. So I say once again, you're welcome."

"It must have been easy for you to write a puff piece on Bill Ruby since you are so in love with him."

Amy had her mouth open to yell a comment back, but he'd sounded jealous when he said that, and it stopped her in her tracks. She hadn't come here to argue. She wanted to see Matt once more and to complement him on finishing his novel, and to confess about writing the article. She should have let it all go, but something drew her here to say goodbye.

"What's been so hard about your month?" she asked.

Matt sat on the couch and put his face in his hands. His voice was muffled. "Sarah broke up with me."

Amy whispered, "Sarah broke off the engagement?"

"When I told her I had kids, she didn't take it well."

"So you believe that they're your boys?"

Matt pointed at the side table where the results to the DNA test were. Amy walked over and picked them up, moving through the pages. She hadn't read the copy that Gary gave her because she thought if she saw the actual evidence, she would end up hating Matt.

"I think the white light in the airplane was my life flashing before my eyes." Matt said as he walked to the kitchen.

Amy could hear glasses clanking as she stared at the papers. It was official, and they both had the scientific proof to show that they were truly the boys' parents. Amy didn't know how or why, but she felt that it was right.

Matt returned from the kitchen with two glasses of whiskey and handed one to Amy. They slugged it down and Amy put the papers and her glass on the table. Matt and Amy stood staring at each other. Amy thought of their kiss in the street, and she wished they could figure this out, but her crush on him was fading with his reaction to the boys. She'd liked Matt for so long, even secretly felt she was in love with him, but she was leaving.

She tried to say something and then shook her head. Almost every waking moment, Amy had thought about how the boys had come into her life, and no matter how she directed her thoughts, there was only one conclusion she could draw.

"I love the boys, Matt, and I think the flash of light must have been God giving us a gift," Amy said in all sincerity.

"I think it was aliens," Matt quipped, and Amy felt flush with regret. He infuriated her, and she wanted to start yelling again. Instead, she turned and stormed out, leaving the front door hanging open behind her.

~

WHEN REYNOLDS LEFT HIS APARTMENT, Matt said good riddance, and then he paced the floor through the night. Reynolds was infuriating on every level. She claimed that she had gotten him the interview job with Bill Ruby, she wrote the article, and then made him feel like a schlep just because he didn't welcome three strange boys into his home. She was crazy!

By midnight, Matt was unhinged. He thought about Sarah and the future they were supposed to have together, and he couldn't believe it was lost. He should have begged Sarah to stay with him. He regretted showing her the DNA test results. He reasoned that he could have denied anything she might have heard.

Everything he had been working toward had been undone by the Bermuda Triangle. He'd actually finished the first draft of his novel, and he couldn't focus on his accomplishment. Out of college, being an author was the dream, and then the access and glamour of Sarah had been the dream, and now Reynolds had become the nightmare.

Reynolds hadn't even commented on his novel and between arguments with her, he'd forgotten to ask if she'd read any of it. He wasn't certain why he'd sent it to her but for the fact that she was the only one who even knew he was working on it.

Somewhere near the middle of his bottle of whiskey and four in the morning, Matt had fallen asleep face down on the couch.

Matt had a recurring dream at least eight separate times in the last two years. He was at a beautiful house that was built right on the ocean. The massive doors to the patio were slid wide open and guests gathered around him in the great room. Everything in the room was white from the walls to the decor. It was his house, and he was rich and famous.

Matt sauntered around the room sipping on expensive bourbon and feeling significant. There was a comfortable white armchair and Matt sat down, letting his leg hang over the side. He was important and he knew it.

When he sat in the chair, all of the guests became red helium balloons that floated to the ceiling, and it was only Matt left in the room among the streamers that hung down from each balloon. His fulfilled smile turned to a gray feeling of loneliness, and he sat in the white chair and finished his drink utterly alone.

Matt sucked in air when he woke, a pool of drool on the leather cushion wetting his cheek. It was sunny and he didn't want to open his eyes. His sticky cottonmouth reminded him that he'd drank too much, and all of the complaints of last night flooded back in, and then he remembered his dream.

He sat up on the couch and felt guilt rising in his throat. He couldn't imagine why at first, and then a feeling of clarity overcame him. Matt finally deciphered his recurring dream. He saw that his vision of success was a trap, and all of the guests in the room were full of hot air, not really interested in Matt as much as they were interested in his success. He realized that even Sarah would have been someone floating off to the ceiling as an empty promise. In his dream, he had the fancy house and all of the spoils, but his life was empty. Matt was astonished to realize that his dream was his subconscious showing him his empty future.

Matt popped some aspirin and showered, resolving to start his life over from today. He would get what work he could to pay for his apartment, and he would pursue writing. He wasn't sure how to approach Reynolds, but he would go see the boys to find out what kind of father he might become. A rising feeling of certainty brought a warm glow to the center of his chest. It was a feeling he'd never had before, and Matt knew he was making the right decisions.

An hour later he found himself on the steps of Reynolds' brownstone talking to himself. He was nervous to see the boys. He felt like a father in the waiting room at a hospital, pacing back and forth and waiting for the news. The difference here was that he'd already met the boys on Ruby Island. He wished he'd paid closer attention to them at the time, and he resolved to never make that mistake again.

He was also dreading what Reynolds would say. He'd not forgotten that he'd kissed her in the street, or the look of disappointment on her face when she'd left his house yesterday.

"Well, hello," he heard as the door swung open. Matt froze and looked up. "I'm Mabel. We met last year when you dropped by to pick up the photos from the Arctic trip." She held her hand out, and Matt walked up the stairs and shook it distractedly. He gulped at his moment of truth.

"Is Reynolds here?"

"I thought you'd never ask. You've been out here for twenty minutes."

"Are you going out?" Matt asked. Mabel was dressed in a circa 1970's ladies light pink skirt suit complete with round cap. It reminded Matt of old stewardess uniforms he'd seen in movies.

"Not right now," she answered absently. "Are you coming in?"

Matt tried to smile as he followed Mabel in and closed the door. He stepped into the large front room expecting to see the boys, but it was empty.

"Are the boys here?" he asked.

Mabel smiled and patted him on the shoulder. "I knew you'd come around."

Matt shrugged sheepishly.

"And you don't remember anything about the island either? Those boys are such a strange miracle," Mabel said, waving her hand and leading Matt to the hallway. "You remember the dark room from last time you were here?"

Matt nodded and moved down the hall to the room on the

right. He stepped in, noticing the twin bed in the corner. He wondered if Reynolds was so into her work that she was sleeping in here, or if they needed the room now that the three boys had moved in.

"Reynolds?" he asked as he moved around the counter and ducked below some of the hanging photos. He was alone in the room, and he shrugged. He turned to leave but stopped when he noticed that he was in some of the photos that were hanging over the countertops. He had barely recognized himself.

Matt was standing next to a palm tree with two boys, his beard fully grown. He was wearing a pair of dilapidated shorts and no shirt, and he looked thin but very fit. He and the boys were smiling, holding up five large fish on a stick.

Matt exhaled fast, like he had been punched in the gut. He remembered that day and the fire and eating the fish. Benji had just been born, and Amy was nursing him. Steven who typically ruined the fishing with the busy noise of a small boy had said he wasn't the baby anymore, and he fished quietly that day. They'd made a large haul and celebrated.

Matt thought about Steven and the way he tried so hard to live up to William's expectations as a big brother. They were grown up now and so self-sufficient, although Benji was the baby and he'd taken longer to catch on to everything because Amy doted on him.

Benji, his baby boy, who had learned to read and write faster than the other boys. Amy taught the boys to read with the magazines and manuals they'd found on the airplane, and she taught them to draw letters and words in the sand.

Matt moved from picture to picture rubbing the tears from his eyes as a full lifetime of memories came back to him. Thirteen years that had been lost in time came flooding in at once, and Matt felt such joy and pride. He was a good father, and he loved his sons. There he was holding William as a baby, and there he was weaving palms the way Amy had shown him for a fishing basket. There he was showing William how to use the sharp rocks to make a spear, and there he was cooking a bird over a fire.

More and more memories appeared in his consciousness, like a dying man whose life was flashing before his eyes. Matt couldn't help himself, and he picked up a stack of photos from the counter and looked at the next picture and then the next, and the memories flooded in from all parts of his brain. It was overwhelming. He remembered falling in love with Amy, and the boys' births and how hard it was to make fire and how wonderful it was to lay with Amy under a blanket of unending stars.

He remembered the conversations they had about the boys growing up without a chance at finding love, and their second attempt to repair the aircraft to try to fly back to civilization. He remembered the dread and the exhilaration when the engines started. They would leave the island and the little piece of the world they had carved out, but the boys would have a better future in civilization, and they both knew it.

Matt was flooded with sentiment. All of the memories sat as a lump in his throat. It wasn't long after the crash that he'd given up on making it off the island and his attentions had turned toward Amy. She put him off by reminding him that he was engaged, but in time she stopped talking about Sarah and being rescued, and they shared long glances at each other. Staying alive was grueling work, but they adapted together and found adventure in their work.

He recalled the first time he had reached out and touched Amy's hair, and she had been willing to receive his touch. He could see in her eyes that she had been waiting a long time for that moment. He reached around her waist and pulled her in and kissed her, and his whole life changed. It was more than being trapped on this island. He knew real love for the first time in his life.

Matt picked up more photos and started to laugh and cry at

the same time. This was his life, his real life. It was all Amy. The world, his love, his time, it was all for her. He remembered when Amy told him that she'd had a crush on him since they first met. They'd known each other for two years before the island and had been on several trips together, but she'd never let on. He was flattered and stunned, and he pestered her for not saying anything. She was right as usual, though, and he wouldn't have seen the real her in New York City.

Matt's heart was filled with love for Amy and for the boys. They were his life, and he had to tell them that he remembered it all.

"Amy!" Matt called from the dark room. He picked up a photo of them together on the island from just before William was born. They were in love, and it was apparent in the photo. He was disgusted with his behavior over the last month and he wondered what Amy must think of him. He'd abandoned his own family for a life of frivolity.

"Bill, Steven, Benji!" he called as he moved to the front room.

"They're not here," he heard behind him, and he turned back to the kitchen.

"Where are they?" he asked Amy's mother who was standing still by the counter, her gloves still perched in her hand as though she was going out for an afternoon cocktail.

She ascertained the change in Matt immediately, and a smile crossed her face. "You remember then?"

"I remember," he said, wiping his wet face. "I remember everything, Mabel, you wonderful mother-in-law!" Matt grasped Mabel in a hug that turned out awkward because she didn't move her arms to hug him back.

"Where are they? When do you expect them home?"

"I don't quite know," Mabel told him. "They left this morning for Ruby Island."

CHAPTER 20

he trip to Ruby Island felt long to Amy. Although, a couple of hours were shaved off the normal trip time because they took Bill's private jet straight from New York to the small North Eleuthera Airport. From there, they were transported via Bill's smaller yacht to the island.

When they arrived via Jeep at the house, Amy was expecting to see Donnelly waiting for them at the front door, but Bill Ruby stood there with his tanned and magnificent smile, his white tank top showing off the ripped muscles in his shoulders and arms.

He could give Adonis a run for his money, Amy thought.

Benji and Steven jumped out of the car to give Bill a hug. William followed slower, but he respectfully shook hands with Bill.

"What are you doing here? You said you were going to be on set for the next few weeks." Amy gave Bill a quick hug as the butterflies turned to rocks in the pit of her stomach. She knew why he was here, and he really wasn't going to make this easy.

He said sheepishly, "I just wanted to make sure everything was all set for you and the boys. A category two hurricane is going to

199

pass by in the next couple of days, but it should roll by without much damage. This house is a fortress, and you'll be just fine."

Amy wasn't worried. She had been here before during a category two hurricane, and it had seemed to her like a very bad storm with the high winds, but the island was buttoned down and it passed by without much concern. The storm now moving over the Atlantic Ocean had yet to make category one.

"Thank you, Bill. You're always so sweet to me." She touched his arm and Bill took Amy's hand as they followed the boys into the house. Amy closed her eyes as they walked. She was certain that she knew why Bill was here. She could read him, and she knew what she must do.

Amy stopped walking and put her hand over her face but didn't let go of Bill with her other hand. She laughed at herself and then looked at Bill who was smiling. He rubbed her shoulder, and she sighed.

"What is wrong with me?" she asked rhetorically. She didn't understand why she didn't want to be with Bill Ruby. He was the man stepping up. He was the man that would be a father to these boys. But she knew in her heart that, just like last time, it wouldn't work for her.

Her life had been this way before. She had liked boys who in the end didn't stay with her, and she had dated boys who it turned out she didn't want to be with. Such was the human heart.

She would have to let Bill down, and she felt silly for it. He was literally the American Dream Man, and she was certain that she was a fool. But she couldn't live without the all-in kind of love that she knew was for her, and Bill's celebrity lifestyle wasn't sustainable to Amy.

"Bill, I'm not ready," Amy whispered.

"Listen, Amy, I know you still have a lot to figure out. I'm not pushing. We can take as much time as it takes."

"I do have a lot to figure out, but Bill, you and me is not one of them." She looked down at the floor. "I'm sorry, but I can't."

Bill's hand gently touched Amy's chin so he could see her eyes. She was ready to cry because she did love Bill in a way, just not enough to live in the limelight of his millions of fans. She loved him, for his energy and his generosity, but it wasn't deep enough for her to commit her life to.

"We are so good together, Amy. I love you and the boys. I want to make this work. What can I do?"

Amy shook her head.

"There's something, Amy. We're right for each other. I think we're perfect together."

"Well, you might be perfect, but I have a long way to go," Amy chuckled. She was overwhelmed and Bill wasn't helping. "Please, Bill."

"I will fight for you, Amy. You see me, the real me, and I can be myself around you. I need to fight for that."

Amy smiled and touched Bill's cheek. "I don't think that you should have to fight for love. Don't settle for me, Bill."

"I'm not settling," he said with all sincerity. Amy knew that he wasn't, and it made her feel an inner confidence to know someone as wonderful and handsome as Bill Ruby truly loved her. But she couldn't live on his love alone.

Amy shook her head, and Bill nodded and hung his head in resignation.

Amy whispered, "Please don't let this ruin our friendship, Bill. You're wonderful, and I need you. I just can't be the girl on your arm. It's too big of a space for me to occupy."

Bill stared at Amy and then got a faraway look in his eyes aimed over her shoulder, and she turned to see if there was someone standing behind her.

"What? Do I have something on my face?"

Bill laughed. "Oh man, Amy. I just got it. I'm the guy in the movie."

"What? What guy in the movie, Bill? You're in a lot of movies."

Bill walked to the window of the foyer, one hand running

through his tightly cropped hair. "I'm the guy in love with the girl who is in love with someone else."

Amy blushed and tried to smile, but she didn't know how to feel. She wasn't in love with Bill, and she didn't want to think about the possibility that she even liked Matt as a fellow human anymore. She could see that Bill never thought for a moment that she wouldn't choose him, and she felt sorry that she didn't want this relationship.

"I mean, I knew that you wanted Matt to step up and be a father to the boys, but I never realized seriously that you were in love with him."

"I'm not in love with Matt," Amy squealed in such a high-pitched voice that even she didn't believe herself.

"Ouch, this hurts even more the second time," Bill said as he put his hand over his heart. He paced for a minute and Amy waited, not wanting to argue.

"Donnelly," Bill called and a side door in the foyer swung open. "Is Gary around?"

"Yes, sir," Donnelly said, and he closed the door behind him and moved toward the back of the house.

"Gary's here?" Amy asked.

"We both arrived last night," Bill said, and Amy nodded.

"Gary said that the moment I realized you weren't in love with me, I had to call him."

"You had a bet?"

"It wasn't a bet, really. He told me something about ones and zeros and well, whatever." Bill came toward Amy and put his hands gently on her arms and looked into her eyes. "Amy, I think we are perfect for each other, but..."

He stared at Amy for a long time, but she didn't speak up. She watched his face go from complete self-assurance and love to a moment of confusion, and then to the perfect closed-mouth smile that he used in public. Amy was certain there was never a bad photograph of Bill taken, and he tried not to let his disappointment show even now.

"Amy, my love," Gary said as he walked in and crossed the room to kiss Amy on the cheek.

"Yeah, hi Gary," Amy said, feeling embarrassed about the whole situation.

"Gary, it happened. I figured it out. She doesn't love me," Bill said directly.

"Congratulations," Gary said to Amy, stepping fully between her and Bill. "I told you Amy, it's binary, and I'm so happy that you figured out what you want."

"I..." Amy sputtered as Gary hugged her tightly.

Then Gary winked at Amy and turned to Bill and put his hands on both shoulders. "Bill, we all love Amy, but there is someone out there for you, someone perfect, and we will find her."

"Thanks, man," Bill said, and he nodded with his eyes closed for a second. Amy could tell that he was hurting, but he was Bill Ruby and he wasn't going to wallow, at least not in front of anyone else.

"I see it now, Amy," Bill said. "When you guys flew to the island, how you looked at him."

"I didn't look at him. How did I look at him?"

"You're in love with him, and you were even back then. I lost you before I even had a chance."

"We had just been through something traumatic, Bill," Amy defended, although in her heart, she knew he was right.

"And the way you hesitated letting me take the boys to the game. It wasn't because you were worried about the boys so much. You were worried because Matt's a huge Yankees fan and you wanted him to take the boys to their first game."

Amy bit her lip. "Really, I don't know about that."

Bill smiled. "Come on, Amy. They talked the whole game about what a big Yankees fan their dad is, and they knew more Yankees history than Jennie and DD in the box next to mine. That's unheard of, especially when you add in the fact that the boys were raised on a secluded island and had never seen a game before."

Amy bobbed her head. "I'm sorry, Bill. Gary's right, there is someone out there for you."

"I don't know anyone who's going to see me and not my stardom." He wasn't complaining, it was just a fact of his life.

"I did, Bill, and someone else will too."

"Well," Bill said, sighing and patting Amy on the shoulder. "I'm headed to work. You and the boys stay and enjoy the island for as long as you want, and Donnelly can help you with anything you need."

Amy didn't want to take advantage. "I don't know, Bill."

Bill sighed. "I think we are meant to be in each other's lives for some reason, Amy. Just take a vacation. You're already here, and the boys love it." Bill put his hands palms out. "I won't push anymore," he said, and Amy's smile was his answer.

AMY LAY on the veranda and looked out over the ocean. Ruby Island was beautiful and she was glad that she and the boys had come back for a week or two of vacation. The boys liked the excitement and grandeur of New York City, and they loved Mabel, but Amy wasn't sure if that was where she wanted to settle down.

She needed Mabel now more than ever, and she had grown up there, but she wasn't sure if it was the place for her boys. They thrived here on Ruby Island. They chased animals and set traps, truly enjoyed the ocean for swimming and fishing, and they seemed more suited for a life in the outdoors.

Amy sighed and sipped her iced tea as she watched the boys play in the low surf. She would be leaving Manhattan behind, and leaving Matt behind forever. Even though she'd never really had a relationship with Matt, or at least remembered having a relationship with Matt, she felt heartbroken. She still savored the memory of their kiss, but she was so disappointed in him, and it was a feeling that was hard to overcome.

They were friends, and she always knew in her heart that he was a good man. She could see now that it was her vision of Matt that was the good man, not Matt himself. The fact that he could abandon their boys, even knowing that they were his sons with the absolute proof of the DNA tests, was unconscionable.

Amy bit her lip, and she watched the emotion pass through her like someone would watch a cloud float by in the sky. All of her wants toward Matt were fading fast and she couldn't invest in her feelings for him anymore. She could only look to the future. She could only look to the beauty of the sunset and be glad that she could see what was important, even if Matt could not.

Amy tipped her head back and looked to the sky. She enjoyed watching the dark clouds roll in. Threats of a hurricane would bring a horrid storm, but it was somehow beautiful to watch the far-off darkening clouds in the still calm breeze. She heard the buzzing engine of a motorboat in the distance and turned her head to the dock, assuming it was the boat returning with supplies from the mainland and readying to take Bill back to the airport.

$\mathcal{M}$att had spent the last twenty-four hours traveling. He'd gone to pick up his passport and a change of clothes at his apartment and booked the first flight he could find to Miami. Matt needed to get to his family. He'd been away from them for a month, and before that he'd only missed one day in his boys' lives. He'd gone searching for fruit and the off chance a ship was passing, and a storm had brewed up quickly. He was trapped on the other side of their small island to weather the storm. He'd raced back as fast as the terrain would allow and was relieved to find Amy and their babies safe. William was seven by then, and Benji was just a baby.

Matt needed to race to them now. He choked on the panic that was rising in his throat. He tried to keep calm in the airport because he didn't want to get flagged and removed from his flight. He thought he could get to Ruby Island in ten hours, and still that was too long.

Matt stared out the window and remembered everything. He had landed on the small island where by some miracle, there was just enough open beach to touch down. But the sand was soft and the landing gear and the left aileron had broken. He and Amy were mostly unscathed, and they filled the next two days bickering and waiting for the rescue that would never come.

Amy had been resilient for the first two weeks, foraging for food and water, and generally using every skill she had studied when she was going on remote photo shoots. Matt felt like he hadn't paid attention to anything that mattered in life before now. He made fun of her, calling her a geek several times, but stopped when she wouldn't share her food with him. He was the big strong man who was behaving like a child, and Amy wasn't having it.

They became a good team in the daily chores of keeping alive. Matt had been able to start a fire to help cook what bird or fish they might catch, and he'd made a small shelter next to a rock overhang after the first bad storm they had weathered inside the airplane. The wind had hammered them so hard that he was worried the plane might flip over into the sea.

Matt's crush on Amy formed rapidly, and he chastised himself for turning against his fiancé so quickly. He had loved Sarah, but the weeks he'd spent with Amy were life-changing. He'd thought she was cute, but he'd never really gotten to know her past their current assignment and spending time badgering her. He counted her as a friend before they became stranded, but he was seeing a whole new side to her.

Amy had kept her distance, but after two weeks of toughing it out, she broke down and cried and allowed Matt to hold her as she rattled through all the reasons they would never be saved. She was convinced they were going to die tired and alone. That was the first time Matt wanted to kiss Amy, but when she looked up and noticed him watching her, she'd pulled away and started talking about Sarah.

They were always exhausted with physical work, but two months in, they had callouses on their hands and feet, and the business of staying alive was coming more natural to them. Matt had forgotten about their old lives and was only interested in

Amy giving him a moment's time. She was always bustling about, going to the small stream they had found with the empty water bottles to refill them, tidying up, or trying to make a basket with palm fronds.

"You're like a robot, Reynolds," he told her as he followed her to collect bananas.

"We're alive, aren't we?" Amy didn't even stop to have a conversation, and it was like torture.

"Am I so bad that you won't even look at me? I'm tired of talking to your back."

"What?" she'd yelled and turned back to look at Matt. Her face was indignant, but he could see her blush.

"Why won't you talk to me anymore? What did I do to make you hate me?"

Matt watched Reynolds cry right then and there, looking at him and wiping the tears from her face, but not saying a word. They stared at each other for a long time, and then he walked to her, pulled her close and kissed her for the first time. She didn't push him away, and that began their twelve-year love affair. Amy admitted to him hours later that she'd had a crush on him since they had met, and she felt trapped because he was engaged to another woman.

"I have ended my engagement. I ended it two weeks after we landed here. I can't think of anyone else but you, Reynolds."

It was a fast affair from there. They were in love with each other, stranded together on a tropical island, and they had the hope of a lifetime together, however long that might be.

Matt rubbed his eyes and let the memories come back. He arrived in Miami in early evening, but his flight was late and he waited twelve hours for the next flight to Eleuthera Island. Matt was at his wits end, and he opted to sleep in the airport in case by some miracle someone decided to go to the island overnight. He never would have slept on a hard airport floor before, but now he could remember sleeping in the back of the cramped aircraft, on the sand, on the giant palm bed he'd made, and on the flat rocks near the shore, and the thought of comfort had changed for him.

When he finally got to Eleuthera Island, he caught a ride to the nearest dock and then made the mistake of hiring the first ferry he saw to try to get to Ruby Island. The man took Matt east and halfway around the island only to let Matt off at the dock where Bill Ruby's boat parked.

Matt argued with the ferry captain that he wanted to go directly to Ruby Island, only to be left behind and told that only one boat on Eleuthera went to Ruby Island, and that was Bill Ruby's boat. Matt tried to board that boat only to be told that no one that wasn't on the list got to Ruby Island. He'd called Amy's cell phone about a thousand times but it went straight to voicemail. He was desperate to get to Amy and the boys, and nothing was going his way.

I deserve it, he thought, as he remembered the times Amy had tried to talk to him about the boys in the past month. He was so stubborn and focused on the wrong future. Matt made a mental note to thank his dad for pushing him toward his family.

Matt asked six boat captains to take him to Ruby Island, but each told him that they couldn't go there without permission. He tried offering up to one thousand dollars, but still there were no takers. The seventh boat owner had a small dinghy, and he said he'd make some calls. After fifteen minutes of waiting, he returned and took Matt's picture with his cell phone, which annoyed Matt to no end. He was trying to smile a harmless smile, but he was thinking if he got to Ruby Island, he would strangle Bill Ruby.

Finally, the man invited Matt to climb down into his small boat. Matt offered money, but the captain turned him down.

"Bill Ruby will take care of everything," the man said in Bahamian accented English.

It took five minutes for Matt to realize that Ruby could have allowed Matt on his yacht instead of making him risk his life in this tiny boat. But Matt understood because he wouldn't fight fair to win Amy over either.

He watched the sky darken and took solace in the weather report that the center of the storm was still more than a day out. Matt almost threw up countless times though, as the waves threw the small boat around and the whine of the small engine screamed in his ears. Forty minutes later, he was relieved to see the mansion on Ruby Island off in the distance, and he wondered if Bill would have his huge security guard throw him in the ocean.

Finally, they were tied up to the dock and Matt saw he was correct. Bill's menacing bodyguard with huge arms and long dreadlocks was waiting for him. There was a golf cart parked by the dock, but the bodyguard stared at Matt and pointed toward the house, and Matt was made to walk. The guard stayed back presumably to pay the boat pilot.

Matt was in the same slacks and long sleeved shirt with jacket that he'd worn to go see Amy at her house, and he was soaked through with sweat when he reached the front door. He stood there dumfounded for a minute looking for the doorbell, but there was none. He was reaching out to knock when the door opened.

"Oh, Mr. Cole, you're back," the butler Donnelly said dryly.

Just then, Blondie walked by with a travel bag and held his hand out to shake Matt's hand. Matt should have guessed that this tanned and platinum blond beach-dweller was Bill Ruby's henchman. Even though Matt should have been thanking him for forcing the DNA test, Matt's first instinct was to kick him where it would hurt the most.

Blondie smiled wide. "Hey, it's been a while, Matt."

Matt deadpanned, "It hasn't been long enough."

"Good one, mate," Gary said, and when Matt didn't shake his hand, he patted Matt hard in the shoulder where he'd stuck the needle before. "Be good to her. Amy is someone very special."

"What do you know about Amy?" Matt said with a hard stare. No one knew his wife like he did.

"Matt, what's the occasion?" he heard. Bill Ruby stepped out and sized Matt up at the door. Matt saw two men moving out the side door to load luggage into the Jeep.

"Going somewhere?"

"How did you get here?" Ruby asked with a 'cat ate the canary' smile on his face.

"Thanks for buying off all the locals."

"Where did you park your dinghy? I'll make sure it finds the bottom of the ocean like your airplane."

"Good one, Bill," Blondie laughed.

"Where are Amy and the boys? Mabel said they're here." Matt looked over Ruby's shoulder but he didn't see or hear anyone in the house. Bill Ruby looked at Matt with his steely-eyed stare, and Matt wondered if he was going to have to force his way in.

"Be good to her," Bill Ruby said, his eyes changing to the faraway slits of someone deep in thought.

"Why does everyone keep saying that? She's my wife!"

Bill Ruby shook his head. "Well, I don't know about that, but she's in love with you, Matt. Don't be an idiot and screw this up again."

Ruby nodded at Donnelly and then stepped around Matt, heading to the Jeep with Blondie. Matt watched the choreographed ballet as the rest of the men waited to see which seat Bill Ruby would take before entering the car and driving toward the launch.

Donnelly led Matt through the house to the veranda overlooking the ocean. Matt saw the boys playing in the surf, and he dropped his coat and his bag and ran across the grass and sand to meet them. He ran right into the surf in his shoes and pants and scooped Benji up and swung him around.

"Daddy, Daddy!" Benji screamed and laughed as Matt swung him around and around. Steven and William heard Benji and then stopped playing and watched. Matt looked at his boys, and he could see that they were tentative about him, and it broke his heart. He'd abandoned his sons for over a month, and he was ashamed.

"Steven," Matt said, and the boy ran to him and hugged him around his stomach. Matt leaned down and kissed Steven's head, reaching his free arm out to William. His eldest son walked over in the surf and took Matt's hand, shaking it firmly.

"I love you, son," Matt said to William with tears in his eyes. "I love you all, and I owe you an apology."

"Do you remember the island, Dad?" William asked.

"I do, son. I remember everything. Where's your mother?"

William pointed back at the house, and Matt could see Amy reclined in a patio chair watching intently. He'd run right past her when he'd seen the boys.

"I'm going to go talk to your mother," Matt said, putting Benji back in the water.

Matt walked slowly back up to the house. His heart was pounding and he had a million things to say to Amy, but he wasn't sure where to start. He saw her stand up; her beautiful form frozen and tentative. When he stepped onto the brick patio, Matt crossed to Amy and pulled her into his arms and kissed her. Amy was stunned.

"I love you, Amy, I always have. Well, at least since we crashed into that stupid, wonderful island."

"You love me? I don't even know if I like you anymore," she said and stepped back.

∼

AMY DID LIKE MATT, though. Since Bill had said goodbye, she'd been sitting out here watching the boys and thinking about Matt. If she'd admit it, she'd thought about him non-stop for the last two years.

"I'm really mad at you, Matt," she said, pounding him in the chest and pulling away.

"You should be, Amy. I'm so sorry. I don't know what else to say except I will do my best to make it up to you. We love each other."

"You remember the island?"

Matt nodded and smiled. "It was wonderful, Amy."

"Well, I don't remember anything." She crossed her arms, which forced him to let go. Amy didn't know if she was more upset that he'd abandoned them or because he could remember and she couldn't. It was easy to love her three sons, but very hard not remembering any of their childhoods.

"It will come back to you, I know it will."

Amy shook her head.

"You love me, Amy," Matt told her with such certainty that she wanted it to be true, but she was so confused and she didn't know where to start.

Amy blushed. "I don't think I do."

"You told me that you always had a crush on me, Amy."

She looked up into his eyes. It just dawned on her that he'd called her Amy four times now, and she wasn't sure if he'd ever used her first name before. "You called me Amy."

"I always call you Amy."

"No, you always call me Reynolds."

"I've called you Amy since the night we were married. It was a destination wedding. Just you and me under the stars on our beach with the sound of the waves and the breeze through your curls."

Matt stepped forward to tuck Amy's hair behind her ear and

it felt familiar to her, although she was certain that he'd never done that before.

"Your hair kept blowing into your eyes just like this." Matt put his hands on her shoulders, and Amy swallowed back her tears. He was saying everything she ever wanted to hear, but it didn't seem real and she wasn't sure how to react.

"Your name is Amy Cole, and you are my wife. It's you and me, it always has been. I'm so sorry that I didn't remember. I didn't know any of it. I didn't remember how much I love you and the boys. Please, Amy. You have to remember," he pleaded.

Matt looked as though he could cry, and she didn't know what to do. She wanted to believe him, but she had no memory. Amy looked down the beach at the boys who were now standing on the sand and watching their parents attentively. The boys remembered, and she'd seen the photo proof, but she couldn't will her brain to remember.

"Matt, I think I was in love with the crush that I had on you and not the real you. I don't think I really knew you at all, and now I have the boys to worry about. I don't know what to say."

"You said the same thing on the island, that you were in love with the crush you had on me and the person you had made me in your mind. Don't be in love with the person you had a crush on, Amy. Be in love with me. Even if you don't remember our life together, me and the boys do. And you took all of those wonderful pictures. I wish I saw those a month ago. I wish I remembered because then I wouldn't have behaved like such an idiot."

Matt took Amy's hands and she looked at her hands in his. He was leaning down and looking straight into her eyes, and she could tell that he was sincere.

"Matt, I..." she stuttered and shook her head. Amy knew she loved Matt, she had since she'd first laid eyes on him, but it seemed like it was just too late. "Matt, I don't have any memories from the island. I admit that I had a crush on you, but that was before."

Matt nodded and dropped her hands, walking away slowly and rubbing his hands through his hair. Amy realized that she felt disappointed that he was giving up on her. She put her hand to her forehead and whispered, "What do I want?" She wanted to scream at him and at herself. It was impossible to figure out what she wanted when she'd wanted him for so long, and she'd given up.

When she looked up, Matt was standing in front of her with an easy smile and the gleam of tears in his eyes.

"I can tell you anything you want to know, Amy. I can tell you that you cried when you realized you were pregnant, but even more when you had Steven because you always wanted a sibling. I can tell you that you are really bad at fishing, but you will do it to eat, and you always apologize to the fish."

Amy nodded. "I did want a sibling."

"I wonder what it would be like to make a specific decision about your life, of the path you want to follow, and to be absolutely sure about your path, and to know that you are exactly right about it"

Amy retorted defensively, "You seemed pretty confident that you were headed in the right direction, and that road didn't include us."

"Wait, let me finish," Matt said patiently. "If one chose their life's direction only to get to the very end of life to see where they made mistakes. To look back and see where you took the wrong turn. It would be devastating to have that clarity. To get to the end and to know in your heart exactly where you went wrong. Maybe it would be better to not have seen your mistake."

Amy threw her arms up because she had no idea what he was trying to say.

"Amy, I am that person. I'm so mad at myself that I chose not to be with you when I couldn't remember, and I know that was so clearly a huge mistake. Please hear me now. I love you, Amy. You are my wife. You are the girl from the ice cream shop."

Amy wiped away a tear. "I don't know what that means."

Matt chuckled. "You asked me on the airplane all those years ago right before we crashed. I mean, maybe to you it was just a month ago, but for me it was the day we crashed on the island. You said that I wasn't really in love with Sarah because I didn't love her to the core of my being."

Amy giggled, and she started to sweat. She remembered saying that because Matt had laughed at her statement.

"You asked me what if I got married to her, and in five years I was in an ice cream shop, and the girl of my dreams walked in, what would I do? And I said I would walk away because I was already married, and I would just watch her go. But I don't have to watch her go, you see? You are the girl from the ice cream shop."

Amy was crying now. She had been in love with Matt Cole for too long, and she didn't remember the island or their wedding or the births of their sons, but she knew she would have longed to hear these words two months ago. She knew now that she didn't really understand how deeply she had felt for him. She looked over at their three boys who were walking up the beach, and she knew that she wanted a lifetime with Matt.

"I have very good news, Amy. Your life hasn't passed you by yet. Do you remember your fortieth birthday?" Matt was smiling, but he wasn't toying with her.

Amy patted him in the stomach with the back of her hand.

"Of course you don't, but I do. The boys were sleeping, and I had planned a celebration with that horrid fermented whatever-fruit juice I made, and you couldn't stop crying because you were forty years old and you were sure you had wrinkles on your face that I wasn't telling you about. You were a wreck."

"That's good news?" she asked, her voice cracking.

"Yes, it is good news." Matt stepped forward and took Amy's

hands in his. He leaned down so his face was closer, and he smiled more warmly than she could ever remember. "You are only thirty-two years old, sweetheart. You're not forty yet. You get those years back again."

Matt gently wiped away Amy's tears, and he leaned down to kiss her. They embraced for a long time, and when they finally parted and Amy was giggling, she looked over to see their three boys standing next to them. Matt and Amy pulled William, Steven, and Benji in for a long hug.

"I want a real wedding, Matt, one that I remember. And then you have to dance with Mabel at the reception," Amy said.

"Reynolds!" Matt yelled, and he pulled her in again for another long kiss.

They did get married, and Matt danced with Mabel and then Amy danced with Matt's father at the reception. Amy also danced with each of her sons and Mabel did too. They called her Auntie Mabel, but Amy started calling her mom 'Grandma' when they were alone.

For the rest of their lives together, Amy never did remember their lost years on the island or how they fell in love, and Matt never forgot. She read their whole story when Matt became a best selling author after he published a book about what they lovingly called their 'Ruby Island Incident'.

ALSO BY ANITA RENAGHAN

Jackpot - Reviewed as "Breakfast Club on wheels", five strangers spend the night driving into the midwest countryside sharing introspection, judgment, and their outlook on the future.

Prince S - Book 1: The Avalon Hall Trilogy

King Pawn - Book 2: The Avalon Hall Trilogy

Queen's Call - Book 3: The Avalon Hall Trilogy - A Young Adult Medieval Fantasy Trilogy, Avalon is born a girl but raised as the male heir to the throne. Avalon is a teenager falling in love for the first time amid deception and adventure.

The Suicide Man - A Chicago lawyer with a sad history is on the brink of suicide. Can Hazel save him from himself?

Thanks for reading! If you loved the book and have a moment to spare, I would really appreciate a short review as this helps new readers find my books.

Please go to anitarenaghan.com/books where you can find more titles and join the email list to receive a free ebook.